**MEET NEW YORK'S
SAM BRISCOE.
HE'S STREET-WISE, HARD-NOSED,
AND ALL HEART . . .**

"I knew what they would do because as a reporter I'd seen them do it in a lot of other places. They would examine her broken face and head . . . they would telephone her children . . . and then they would try to find the people who did it to her. And I knew sitting there that I would have to try to find those people too . . . and hurt them a little harder than they'd hurt me, and maybe as hard as they hurt Sarah. I wasn't a cop, but this was family. This was about a nice woman and her once nice husband, and I would have to do something about it, or I would never feel good again."

THE DEADLY PIECE
by PETE HAMILL
Author of DIRTY LAUNDRY

THE
DEADLY
PIECE

PETE HAMILL

THE DEADLY PIECE

A Bantam Book / March 1979

ISBN 0-553-12073-5

Published simultaneously in the United States and Canada

Bantam Books are published by Bantam Books, Inc. Its trade-mark, consisting of the words "Bantam Books" and the por-trayal of a bantam, is Registered in U.S. Patent and Trademark Office and in other countries. Marca Registrada. Bantam Books, Inc., 666 Fifth Avenue, New York, New York 10019.

*This book is for
my daughter Adriene.*

1.

That Thursday night, rain pelted the city, coming off the harbor in gray slanting sheets, driven by a hard autumn wind. The wipers worked furiously, cleaving aside the steady rain, while Sonny Rollins played "Isn't She Lovely" on WRVR. Times Square was almost empty. We stopped for a light at Forty-second Street, and I could see a few long-legged black hookers shivering under the marquee of the Rivoli, and a transvestite in a blonde wig pirouetting in the cold rain, while a mustachioed young cop watched from inside the cigar store on the corner. The cop's face was wreathed by brightly packaged condoms, pale sleek vibrators, mounds of rolling papers, Afro picks and switchblade knives. He stared out at the rain, looking sad enough to cry.

"It's never gonna stop," Marta Torres said, slumping low in the seat beside me. "It's just gonna keep on raining forever, Sam."

"Nah," I said. "Red Emma here would die of a broken heart. She likes the sun. A lousy mudder."

"Leave my mudder out of this."

"I never met the lady."

"Neither have I," she said, and looked out across the square as the light changed.

"Really?" I said.

"Momma left Poppa when I was six weeks old. She went back to the sun and I never saw her again. The only thing she left me was the way I feel about cold rainy nights in New York."

"Well, I guess we'll all have to settle for Ray Barreto, *guapa.*"

Ray Barreto is the best conga player in the universe, and we were going to see him play at Madison Square Garden. Red Emma is my car. She is a Jaguar XJ-5, with V-12 engine, eye-level warning light array and precision cast aluminum inlet manifolds. I don't have any idea what any of those words mean, but I like saying them. It's like an American version of the Rosary. Red Emma was a product of the week of the Big Score, a time in my life when I took home $6,500 in expense money from the fall of Saigon and ran it up to $108,000 at the blackjack tables of Vegas. It was the most money I had ever made and I promptly retired. I never played cards again either, but with the money I bought Red Emma and a custom-designed loft in SoHo. I didn't realize until the first dismal storms of winter that Emma was more Bovary than Goldman, and that deep within her sophisticated exterior beat the treacherous heart of a chorus girl. Emma just didn't stand up: she teased, beckoned, promised and seduced, and she was lousy in mud.

Marta Torres was a Nuyorican, born on One Hundred and Eighth Street and First Avenue in the heart of El Barrio. She went from Washington

Irving High School to Columbia to a fancy Protestant law firm that was integrating the year she graduated from law school. Integrating meant that after eighty-three years of existence, they were taking Catholics. In another eighty-three years, they might start accepting Jews. Marta lasted a year with the chinless wonders downtown, and then went to work for the legal department of one of the few honest poverty programs in the city. That's where I met her, researching a story for a magazine that went out of business a month before the article was supposed to see print. She spent most of her time trying to put landlords in jail and getting poor people out. She was the oldest twenty-six-year-old I knew, and I liked her a lot.

I liked her laugh and I liked her throaty voice and I liked the way she used Spanglish for a staggering variety of freshly minted obscenities. I liked the smell of her in the closed space of the car, a pilgrim mixture of soap and flowers and rain. She was what the Puerto Ricans call a *trigueña*, which means that her skin was the color of burnished copper and she had straight black hair, good white teeth, and the high cheekbones of the Caribbean Indians. I glanced at her hair, gleaming in the lights of the traffic, and I wanted to stop the car and lean over and push my hands through it. I didn't because she would have laughed at me. She laughed at me a lot.

"*Coño*, look at this *mierda*," she said, as we caught up to the traffic on Seventh Avenue. A wall of yellow taxicabs stood between us and the Garden, all glistening in the steady rain, their taillights blinking like a hundred red eyes. "They look like they're on strike."

3

"We'd better walk," I said.

"In this stuff?"

"I'm old. I have to exercise."

"Yeah, and I have to be warm. When it gets too cold, my ass falls off."

"Good grief. Not that."

"I swear."

"In that case, we better go straight to my place, and the hell with the concert."

"I told you, Briscoe. You're too old for me."

"Yeah, but I'm kind, gentle, trustworthy, elegant. I can order wine. I can talk about music and art, Balzac, and Thomas Mann. I . . ."

"Let's walk."

I pulled into a spot beside an all-night cafeteria. The customers were as still as a Hopper painting, frozen to their stools by the chill of the night. I pocketed the keys, found the umbrella on the floor behind the seat and got out. Marta groaned, untangling her long dark-stockinged legs from the small car, and she took my arm and pressed against me with one hard young breast. She smiled and her green eyes twinkled in a teasing way. In heels, she was eye-level with me, and I'm an even six feet.

"You're too tall to be a Puerto Rican," I said.

"I'm not a P.R., schmuck. I'm a Swede. I'm just trying to pass as a P.R."

"Well, you're definitely a wise-ass."

"Hey, you got hard arms."

"It's from lifting Puerto Rican dames over my head."

"How do you do with Swedes?"

"The best I can."

The marquee of the Garden told us that the Fania All-Stars were waiting inside, along with

4

Ray Barreto y su Combo and a group from East Harlem call Tipica '73. They were beautiful musicians, but they were not the main reason we were there. La Lupe was. She was listed as the Extra Added Attraction, and there was a time, not long before, when she had been the greatest female entertainer in the world. Nobody else came close. Not Liza. Not Barbra. Not Shirley. La Lupe was simply incredible. But then something had happened, and her hot roll had broken, and she had vanished for a long time. There were rumors everywhere in the Latin music world: she had made a bad marriage, she was fooling around with drugs; she had gone into *santeria*, a mystical Caribbean cult that requires the women to shave their heads and wear white for a year. I knew her well enough to dismiss the drug rumor; she was reluctant even to use aspirin. But she had gone away, for too long a time, and tonight she was coming back and that was the big reason why Marta and I were walking among the autumn crowds, spattered by the drops of fat gray rain.

"They're looking at you weird, Briscoe."

"Who?"

"My people. They think you're a cop."

"Now that's another reason why the poor are poor," I said. "They're dumb."

"You look like a cop to me."

"I do?"

"A crooked one."

"Jeez, and all along I thought I looked like a rising young archbishop, making his way through Mother Church."

"That's what I mean. A crooked cop."

We moved into the Rotunda, and the crowds

were thicker, as thousands came piling out of the subways to join the rivers of people flowing from massed taxis. All of them were damp with the rain. That year, all the young men were dressed like John Travolta, in tight white suits and polished boots, walking with an insolent grace, wearing their girls like ornaments. But there were older people among them, too, all the dashing young men of 1958, who had worn their one-button rolls and Flagg Brothers shoes to the Palladium, where they did thunderous mamboes that seemed to fracture the world. I knew from the way they walked that the music of Machito and Tito Puente was still playing in their heads, alongside the memories of lost girls and good dope and great drunks and all the other lovely things they did in the years before they got married and had kids and took jobs in places where they didn't care how you danced. The Palladium was the greatest dance hall of its time, and when I was young, I would move back and forth on a summer evening from Birdland to the Palladium, from the music of Dizzy and Bird and Miles, to the timbales of Puente and the dark-eyed girls with roses in their hair. The old boys of the Palladium had a kind of permanent melancholy to them now, as they moved into the Garden to listen to the music that their children called *salsa*; they were as old as I was, but I could see their eyes drifting away from their heavy baby-thickened wives to the fresh, shiny faces of the young Nuyorican girls, the kids born in Rainbow Town, and I realized suddenly that Marta was only nine the year that Jack Kennedy was assassinated and I wondered if she saw in me that

6

same sad and drifting look that I picked up in the aging boys of the Palladium. I started to crack wise, which is what I usually do when something somber has come to life in my head, but I was suddenly bumped aside, almost knocking Marta down.

"Hey!" I said, whirling, ready to defend myself or strike back, when I saw that we weren't the only citizens being shoved around. A flying wedge of men in raincoats and sunglasses was driving through the dense crowd, using shoulders and weight to slice a path to the inside lobby of the Garden. In the center of the wedge were two men I had seen before, in the years when I was still chipping away at vice and folly for a newspaper. The two men were absolutely dry.

"*Monon!*" I shouted, holding Marta's hand. The taller of the two men looked around, without seeing me. His brown lustrous eyes were wary, and he glanced at the shorter man beside him for reassurance. The wedge stalled. People shouted bad words in Spanish. "Monon!" I said. "Over here!"

Monon Perez saw me now, and his tall, powerful body relaxed under the tight-belted raincoat. The squat man beside him put his right hand in the pocket of his gray overcoat. I knew him too. They were some pair. Monon Perez was in his early thirties, with coils of dark hair falling onto his flat brow. He had the sensual lips and dilating nostrils of a man accustomed to violent pleasures, his weight-lifter's body ready to hurt strangers.

"Briscoe, you rat bastid," he said, from twenty feet away. He smiled in an oily way, the lips parting to show teeth but not moving horizontally.

A few years before, I had written some articles about the network of poverty programs he had plundered in Brooklyn; I had listed the politicians he had supported with contributions and field workers; I had related the tale of the way he had consolidated power one hot August night, when his principal rival was run over by a car. Twice. But the smile said that he had survived everything the punks of the press had said about him, and, of course, he was right.

In the street, they called the other one the Turtle. He had been a professional wrestler in the era of Gorgeous George, one of the series of Masked Marvels who had grunted and groaned and faked it for the old ladies in the early days of TV. But the Turtle had no talent for acting. His favorite move was to snap his teeth around your ear and rip. That's why they called him the Turtle. That is also why his fellow actors in the wrestling trade refused to perform with him anymore. So Turtle had wandered from the arenas; had worked as a strong man in a Coney Island flea circus; done some bouncing in a string of cheap Bronx nightclubs; employed his muscle as an organizer for the taxi union; collected for some loan sharks. All the while happily spitting ears on sidewalks. And then he had found his ducal prince in Monon Perez: someone who paid him well and had a limitless network of political connections, which meant a limitless number of friendly judges, bailbondsmen and police captains. Working for Monon Perez, the Turtle never had to restrain himself again.

And now he was staring at me from beyond the hedge of Monon's boys, his eyes the color of slush, his thinning hair pasted to his bullet-like skull and not quite covering the cauliflowered stump that had once been his own right ear.

"Hello, Turtle," I said, as he and Monon came closer and the crowd jammed even tighter at the doors, another fifty feet away. "You look as handsome as ever."

Marta's palm was damp in my hand. Monon got between me and the Turtle.

"Hello, Briscoe," Monon said.

"You stickin' this place up, Monon?" I said. He was close enough now that I could smell his cologne. It was strong and sweet. One of his boys, a thin asp with wrap-around sunglasses, stood between us.

"I came here to be with my people," Monon said, and the lips curled. The asp moved around to my left. I let go of Marta's hand.

"Great," I said. "You can rob them one at a time tonight." The asp was behind me now. "But you better get Turtle to carry the loot. All those nickels and dimes can get heavy, Monon."

He looked at Marta. "You fuckin' her, Briscoe?"

"You got me mixed up with your mother, Monon," Marta said, with a cool smile.

His eyes widened, and then glazed. The right side of his face twitched. I turned to Marta.

"Aw, come on, sweetheart," I said to her. "Don't talk like that. I haven't touched that woman for years."

Monon's head swiveled, glancing around at all the straining Latin faces heading for the door, at the cops guarding that door, at the other cops down at the Seventh Avenue end of the Rotunda. He looked past me, to where the asp was standing. And he turned quickly, and started shoving through

9

the crowd. I scratched my scalp with a finger and braced myself.

"Monon!"

He looked at me again, annoyed, as I scratched away at my scalp.

"Enjoy the show, Monon!"

Then I whipped around and slashed an elbow down at the asp behind me, hitting him in the throat. He backed up, gagging, trying to breathe.

"Oh, I'm so sorry," I said. "Do forgive me. I just didn't realize you were *there*. Had a sudden itch, you see, and —"

Monon had a restraining arm across Turtle's chest. The other asps were all ready to move. But there were more cops now, coming from the side, trying to get the crowd moving. I took Marta's hand again, and tapped the choking asp on the shoulder.

"Frightfully sorry, old chap. Hope you're better. Cheerio."

Then we moved ahead, coming close to Monon again.

"See you around, Monon," I said. He spun away from me, and the flying wedge chopped its way through the crowd to the double doors, and went straight across the lobby to the escalators. They left the asp leaning against a shuttered souvenir kiosk.

"That was beautiful," Marta said.

"Don't encourage me," I said.

"That son of a *puta*, Monon."

"I didn't realize you knew the gentleman."

"Hey, I work for a poverty program. Everybody knows Monon in the poverty business. He's the Rat That Ate Brooklyn."

"Most women think he's a good-looking rat."

"Uck."

We were through the doors now, and I went to Window Seven, where the promoters had left two press tickets. There was a long line waiting for the freebies.

"Who was the other one?" Marta said. "The ice-box with eyes?"

"The Turtle? Just your average card-carrying run-of-the-mill bad guy. He gives good ear. Bites them right off your head."

"I notice you didn't give *him* a shot in the neck."

"How could I? He doesn't have one."

I picked up the tickets and turned left and then I saw Ike Roth. He was twenty feet away, standing in front of a whiskey poster screwed to a beam. Beside him was a large, suety man in a velvet-collared coat. They were not talking. They were waiting. Ike glanced at me through steel-rimmed glasses and then looked away. His bald head was pale blue in the hard fluorescent light of the lobby.

"What's the matter, Sam?" Marta said quietly.

"That guy over there. The bald guy next to the fat one. He's my cousin Ike."

She looked over at Ike. He lit a cigarette and his eyes moved our way. He seemed pale and gray and worried. I smiled at him and he had to smile back. I took Marta's elbow and we walked over. His old middleweight's body set itself, as if expecting trouble.

"Hello, Ike," I said, offering my hand. He shook it and gave me a wan smile. Only the handshake reminded me that Ike Roth was once a tough kid off the streets of Brownsville.

11

"Gee, Sam, I wasn't sure that was you," he said. "You lost some more hair."

"I guess it doesn't run in the family, Ike." I looked at the fat guy, but Ike didn't introduce him. "This is Marta. Marta Torres, my cousin Ike."

They shook hands and he smiled nervously again. I held my hand out to the fat guy.

"Hi, I'm Ike's cousin, Sam."

"Wuddiyuh say."

"He really *is* my cousin, Carmelo," Ike said thinly. "His father and my mother were brother and sister."

Carmelo nodded coldly. I didn't like the thin wire of fear in Ike's voice. It had something to do with this side of beef with the eighteen-inch neck and the blue chin, but I didn't know what it was, except that it was ruining Ike. Carmelo took out a cigarillo, holding it almost delicately between fat thumb and fat forefinger, and then his hooded eyes darted to the outer lobby. A blonde woman in a muskrat coat was moving quickly to the double doors, waving at Ike and Carmelo. Most of the crowd was already inside. Marta seemed puzzled, as if she'd walked into the second act of a play.

"How's the diamond business, Ike?" I said.

"It's great, great. Listen Sam, excuse me, will you?" He smiled bleakly. "This is business, right here." He paused, his eyebrows moving vertically. "It's not what you might think, Sam."

"I wasn't thinking anything, Ike."

He moved across the lobby without saying goodbye, a lean, balding older man now, and the blonde came up to him and kissed him on the cheek. She had a curvy big-assed Latin vulgarity to her, like the girl singers who always worked with Xavier

Cugat. Carmelo didn't move. I took Marta's arm and walked to the escalator that would carry us to the orchestra level.

"What was that all about?" Marta said.

"I don't know," I said. "But Miss Cha Cha of 1969 was definitely not Ike Roth's wife."

"I know," she said. "She's been around for years."

"You know her too?"

"I've seen her around," Marta said, as we went up the escalator. "She was a regular at the Corso for a few seasons."

"The dancehall on Eighty-sixth Street?"

"Right. One season she was a redhead. Another season she turned up with pale blue hair. Her tits were always the same size. Mammoth."

"Ah, jealousy."

"I always say anything over a handful is wasted," she said, smiling. "Anyway, she had the hots for trumpet players. All kinds of trumpet players. But on bad nights she would settle for a timbale player. Or a waiter. Her name is Ileana."

"Ileana what?"

"I don't know. Just Ileana," she said. "One name. Like Charo."

"Or Hildegarde."

"Who?"

"Never mind," I said, feeling old. "Some singer."

"Ileana hasn't been around for a while."

"Maybe she was here tonight to see Carmelo, the large job," I said.

"Are you kidding? She went right to Ike."

"She sure as hell did."

"If it wasn't for the crowd," Marta said, "she might have gone down on him right there."

13

I squeezed her hand. "I know exactly how she felt. I'd like to do something like that right now."

"You're a dirty-minded man, Briscoe. Always making promises."

"I know."

"Well, the hell with the crowd. I can't wait another second."

"Control your lust, girl. Control your lust."

We turned into the orchestra level, and could hear the long, low rhythmic sound of drums. The concert had already begun. I handed the tickets to the red-faced Irish usher.

"How's business?" I said to him.

"Bongo bongo bongo, I don't wanna leave the Congo."

"You mean this isn't the Clancy Brothers concert?" Marta said.

The usher started to say something, but I moved Marta past him toward the drums. She giggled, and then her face was still. She bit the inside of her mouth.

"What business did you say Ike was in?"

"Diamonds," I said.

She looked back down the corridor, and so did I, but there was no sign of Ike Roth and his friends.

2.

The Garden was sold out and I couldn't see the upper balconies in the darkness. I didn't need to. I could hear them and feel them, as they roared for each new act and stomped to the rhythms of salsa, shaking the great building. This was the music of the Caribbean, transposed to New York, pounding and insistent, the music of the *clave*, with congas and bongoes and timbales building the foundations and the brass handling the upper stories. Singers told their stories in *coros*, all about heartless women and faithless women and treacherous women and even an occasional good woman, and all around us, women moved to the music, and their young men were clapping to the one-two, one-two-three rhythm, and the place seemed a long way from the bleak ruins of the South Bronx and El Barrio and the wilds of Brooklyn.

Marta moved with the music too, as if she'd never heard of Columbia University Law School, or courses in Henry James; rising from her seat, her hair snapping from side to side against the rhythm, her sharp hips moving the other way, clapping her hands, chanting the songs. She must have had one terrible time with the downtown Protestants. Years ago, I had danced through a lot of nights in a lot of places, including the old Palladium, learning mamboes of incredible complexity and dancing with girls whose names I never got. But that was all a long time ago, and I didn't dance anymore and was too uptight to get up and just move, and anyway I was looking around for Ike Roth.

"Just let it happen, Sam!" Marta shouted, while Tipica '73 was jamming into second gear. She was standing over me, moving and clapping, and looked taller than ever.

"I'd look like a jackass."

"So what? Who's looking?"

"I'm a reporter," I said sarcastically, "I observe. I don't take part."

"Ah, bullshit," she said, moving to the music, and put thumb and forefinger into her mouth and let out a piercing birdcall, while the building trembled with 19,000 people doing the same thing. Then Tipica '73 finished its set and the few people who were still sitting rose to applaud, including me, and I looked around at all the young faces of the Nuyoricans, that generation that had grown up in New York, spoke English first and Spanish second, and had turned to the music of *salsa* to keep themselves Puerto Rican. And hurrying along the side of the arena, near the exit ramps that led to the dressing rooms, was Ike. I saw a sliver of his face and then he was gone.

"Hey, what's the matter?" Marta said, as Barreto

and his boys came out on stage to set up for the next act.

"Ike. I just saw him."

"So? You saw him in the lobby too."

"Something's the matter. He's in some kind of jam.'"

"So go see him."

"I don't know . . . "

"Don't stand there like a *pendejo*," she said. "You can get me a Coke."

"That stuff makes your face break out, Swede."

"Nothing makes my face break out, Briscoe."

She squeezed my hand as if granting permission, and I edged down the aisle, while a voice announced Ray Barreto. I went to the ramp leading to the dressing rooms. A corridor led away to the left, and a lot of musicians in sequined band clothes were hanging around, smoking and talking to the special cops. Down to the right were rest rooms and a refreshment stand. Ike was leaning on the counter of the stand, drinking beer from a waxed cup.

"Ike . . ."

He whirled, his eyes startled. "Oh, Sam," he said. "Jesus, Sam, uh, hello." And he looked back at the beer. His body had suddenly shrunk, as if to receive a blow, and then loosened to its full size again.

"Christ, Ike, what the hell *is* it?"

"Nothing, Sam. Nothing. Want a beer?"

"Yeah. A beer." He waved at the young waitress. "What is the matter, Ike?"

"Nothing. Nothing. Just business. That's all. Business."

"Where are your friends?"

"Out there."

"I didn't know you liked salsa music, Ike."

"I hate the fucking stuff," he said sharply. Then: "You know me, Sam, I haven't liked anything since Glenn Miller went into the English Channel." He paused. "Like I say. It's business. Tonight's just business."

"Business must be pretty bad."

He gave me a look that said: You don't know the half of it. The waitress brought a beer and Ike gave her a dollar. The music had begun again, and all the way down there in the corridor, I could hear Barreto's congas driving the engine.

"Someday, maybe I'll explain it all," he said.

"Who's the blonde?"

His eyes were wary now. "She's . . . a buyer."

"You're lying, Ike."

"Hey, Sam, I don't have to tell you my life story, you know."

"I know your life story, Ike. I just want to know what's bothering you. You look scared shitless."

He sipped his beer in a sour way.

"I am," he said softly.

There was a great roar from the arena, as Barreto finished his opening number.

"Have you talked to Sarah about it?" I said.

"Wives don't understand—some things."

I couldn't argue that one with him. I'd had a wife once too. She didn't understand a lot of things, most of all, me.

"Want to talk about it later?" I said.

He shrugged. "I'm tied up later."

"What about tomorrow?" I said.

He didn't say anything but he looked at me as if he wanted to talk about everything. I took an index card out of my jacket pocket and wrote my number on it. The one I answered.

"Call me if I can help," I said.

"It's just business, Sam. Really. That's all. Just fucking business."

3.

The Garden was shuddering with applause as I got back to the seat. Barreto was driving hard through the last part of his set, and the sound was enormous. I couldn't get a word out, and Marta just smiled and threw an arm around my shoulders. Finally Barreto finished, to a sustained roar. The musicians took their bows, and started carrying off their instruments, while the stagehands worked on the next act.

"Unbelievable," she said. "His hands are faster now than they were three years ago."

"I heard part of it, under the building."

"So what happened?"

"Nothing yet," I said. "I asked him to call me. He's scared to death."

"If you had to go home with Ileana you might be scared to death too."

"He says it's business."

"Yeah. Monkey business."

Then drums started pounding in the darkened arena, and suddenly the stage was full of smoke and multi-colored lights and there was a long roar and La Lupe was coming out of the smoke. She had lost weight, and was whip-thin in a tight white sheath, her skin dark against the whiteness, and her teeth were flashing and she started singing *"Besitos Pa' Mi"* in her throaty growl and the place went nuts. She panted and teased and screamed, one number working into another, the hair tossing wildly, the hands reaching out for imaginary hair, ears, neck, face, and then the hands were moving over her body, the palms flat against her hips and then rubbing her belly, her tongue flicking along the edges of her lips, and then she was kneading her breasts, first one, then the other, her voice groaning with pleasure, and the Garden groaned with her. Marta was up, moving to the music, high up on her toes, her hips grinding, her tongue moving too, the hair snapping the accents, and I wanted to take her by the hand and take her out of there and go straight down to the loft.

"Lu-pay! Lu-pay! Lu-pay!" the crowd shouted, and she switched into a ballad and calmed them down, and I wondered what Lupe had looked like twenty years before in Havana, when she was a sexy kid singing for sailors and tourists in the Bar Red. She wasn't a kid anymore, and the Bar Red was gone with Batista, and the years had marched across her face as they had with Billie Holiday and Lee Wiley and Anita O'Day. But she looked better now than she had when I'd interviewed her a few years before, and she attacked song after song with a withering carnality that was simple and pure and exhausting.

And then suddenly it was over, and they were putting the lights on in the Garden and everybody was standing and all the young girls were holding

the hands of their boyfriends and Marta was holding mine.

"Now *that's* entertainment," she said, her face
sprayed with a mist of sweat. She smiled at me
lewdly. "Let's get out of here."

"I just have to go back and say hello to La Lupe,"
I said. "She got me the tickets."

Marta looked unhappy. "I'm going too."

"Of course."

"I wouldn't leave you alone with that lady."

"Lupe? She's really a plainclothes nun."

"And I'm Princess Margaret."

"Come on."

There was a big crowd waiting to get into the
dressing room, but one of the trumpet players
recognized me and cleared a path.

"Hey, Briscoe," he said, "how come you don't
write the column for the paper anymore?"

"I got old."

"What?"

Marta smiled at him.

"I don't have the legs anymore. It's like boxing.
You need legs. Mine are shot."

He looked at me in a puzzled way as he shoved
open the door, and we were led into a large room
with a small couch and a dressing table heaped
with flowers. My bouquet stood next to a bunch
from Tito Puente.

"Wait here," the trumpet player said. "She must
be still in the shower."

He went out, and I felt uneasy, and then Lupe
came out of an adjoining room, wearing a white
terrycloth robe, looking small and drained and thin.
She smiled when she saw me and thanked me for
the flowers I'd sent and offered us drinks, and told

Marta to watch out for me, I was too sexy for a nice young girl like her, and then she sat down hard on the couch and lit a cigarette with slow, deliberate movements. I'd seen fighters sit that way in this same building. We talked a little more about the great crowd and how good Barreto was and how more kids were discovering the music every-day and how for them it was always new, and then they were knocking on the door from outside and we exchanged phone numbers and promised to stay in touch. I kissed her on the cheek and she shook Marta's hand and we left.

"You must have had some number with her, Briscoe," Marta said, as we left the crowd and went down the corridor to the exit ramp.

"I never laid a hand on her, I swear."

"You mean you laid two hands on her."

I laughed. "Well, I'll be goddamned! You're jealous."

"Not jealous. Just young and insecure."

"Well, now you know how I ruined my legs."

We went into the arena again. The floor was covered with discarded programs and crushed beer cups and crumpled cigarette packs, and the place looked ugly in the harsh overhead lights. Halfway across the hall, there was a cluster of cops, and two blacks in the white uniforms of hospital orderlies. They were all bending over someone in the seats of the orchestra. I ambled down the aisle, with Marta holding my arm.

"Beat it, pal," one of the cops said.

I fumbled for a press card from my wallet. "Sam Briscoe," I said. "What's going on?"

"A dead guy," he said, looking at the card and then at me. "You lost some hair, huh?"

"Ah, you know. It's the sex-crazed women."

Another cop came over to the first one. "That must have been some concert," he said. "He took one in the heart and nobody noticed."

I pushed past the ring of cops and saw the dead man slumped back in his chair. His jacket was open and there was a large crimson stain spreading on his white-on-white shirt. His overcoat was on the seat beside him and his agate eyes were staring at the ceiling. He was still holding a cigarillo.

It was Carmelo.

4.

     I saw Johnnie Boop standing over on the side, with his broad back against the loge barrier. When I was a kid he ran a bar in Brooklyn that was the Parris Island of drinking; at seventeen, we apprenticed there, and it was survival of the fittest. He liked me because he'd never met anybody else who was half Irish and half Jewish. Now he was the head of Garden security, a big pleasant man who worked every event they put in the building, and knew a lot more about music and basketball and violence than anyone else I knew. We walked over.

     "Hey, Sam, howaya, babe?" he said quietly, looking from me to Marta without moving his head or changing his smile.

     "Hello, John. Who's the stiff?"

     Now he looked directly at Marta.

     "She's okay," I said.

     "His name is Carmelo Fischetti," Johnnie Boop said, gazing around the vast, empty arena, and not moving his lips. "He's a known gambler, as they say, or used to be. He's barred from here during sporting events. I didn't see him come in, 'cause I was straightening out some beef in the balcony. He's carrying heat, but he never had time to use it. A thirty-eight, in an ankle holster. He was whacked out with something small. Maybe a twenty-two. Maybe even smaller. It took one, that's all. Right in the heart. The music must of covered the noise. Tonight, the music could of covered an atom bomb."

"Are they looking for anyone?"

"Who knows?" he said. "Everybody was gone when they realized there was one customer who was never gonna go home alive." He glanced at Marta. "It was probably the usual thing."

"What do you mean?" Marta said.

He didn't answer her. He looked at me. "Skag. Coke. There's a lot of it at these things. I don't mean just the Latin shows. The rock shows are worse. All the little boys and girls come in from Jersey and the suburbs and shove things up their noses. And all the peddlers show up to sell it to them. I couldn't keep track of it all if I tried. I'd have to make arrests with nets."

"Is Carmelo connected?" I asked.

"Oh, he's a wise guy, all right," Boop said, covering his mouth as he lit a cigarette. "But big? A wheel? Nah. This is a small-potatoes wise guy. A hired muscle when he was young. Out of Brooklyn. Then he did some time, and when he got out, he tried to claim a little racket for himself here and there, a couple of jukeboxes, a little dope in a new territory, some shylocking and fencing. The big wise guys let him go his way, 'cause usually he screws it up. But, no," Boop said, and smiled, "he doesn't know Al Pacino personally."

"Thanks, John."

"Anytime, Sam," he said. Then, more openly:

"Hey, you coming to the fights next Friday? That Fallon kid's boxing on top. I hear he's some puncher. Comas in both hands."

"I think I saw him at the Gloves a couple of years ago," I said. "He threw a guy out of the ring. That kid?"

"That's the kid. A crazy Irish bastard."

"If I come, I'll call you," I said.

"See you, Sam."

We walked out through the lobby, where the sweepers were starting to work. Marta was quiet. The rain had stopped, and we walked quickly to the car. The cafeteria was still open and we went inside. I called Harvey Matofsky at the *Post* and told him there was a corpse at the Garden and he should get a reporter and a photographer there in a hurry. I didn't tell him the dead man's name. He thanked me and asked me to come around and talk sometime, because I really should be working on a newspaper. I told him my legs were shot, and he laughed, and I hung up. I opened the door and asked Marta for some dimes.

"Are you trying to impress me with this reporter bit, Sam?" she said. "You don't have to, y' know. I saw all those reporter movies already."

"Just give me the dimes, kiddo."

She smiled and dug some dimes out of her leather bag. I called Queens information and got a number for Isaac Roth in Forest Hills. I dialed and Sarah answered.

"Hello, Sarah. It's Sam Briscoe."

"Why, Sam!" Her voice was round and jolly. "How are you, Sam?"

"I'm great, Sarah. Listen, is Ike there?"

"Why no, Sam," she said, more cautiously now. "He left for San Juan yesterday, on some business thing. Is there anything I can do?"

"Just tell him to call me, if he checks in for messages."

Her voice sounded clenched. "What's it about, Sam?"

"Business."

"Come on, Sam," she said sharply. "Level with me. Is Ike in trouble?"

"He might be."

"Oh, God."

"But he might not be either."

"Oh, God."

"Listen, Sarah, if you get a visit from any cops, I want you to stall them. Ask them if they have a search warrant. If they have one, let them in. If not, play dumb, but let them in anyway. Give them coffee. Give them doughnuts. Sing a couple of songs. But remember: You don't know anything. And call me right away. Do you have a family lawyer?"

"Ike does, but . . ."

"Call him, and tell him to stand by."

"I'll try to find a number for him," she said. "What's this about, Sam?"

"I'm not sure, but it could be about murder."

"Oh, God."

I told her not to worry, gave her my number at the loft and hung up.

Marta was standing there, chewing the inside of her lip, her hands thrust deep into the pockets of her raincoat. A few cabdrivers were drinking coffee at the counter and one weary waitress was smoking a cigarette next to the cash register.

"Let's go to my place," I said.

"All right," she said glumly.

"You don't have to come with me, Marta. I can drive you home."

"I started the night with you," she said. "I might as well finish it with you."

We were deep in the bed in the sleeping loft, her long tawny legs tangled in mine, while Charlie Parker played "April in Paris" from the strings album on the phonograph downstairs, and the rain drummed steadily on the skylight, when the phone rang. Marta sighed and reached for the cigarettes.

"Hello."

"Sam," Sarah whispered. "They're here."

"Did you call the lawyer?"

"I couldn't find him."

"I'll be there as soon as I can get there."

I hung up and looked at Marta. She was sitting up now, smoking, her back against the headboard, her forearms crossing the tops of her drawn-up knees. Her body was dark against the sheets and she let one leg fall to touch the floor as she took a heavy drag. Her face was set somewhere between disappointment and a pout. She looked very beautiful and very young. I glanced at the clock on top of the hardwood dresser. It said 3:10. The cops were working fast. For cops.

"I've got to go over to Queens," I said. "You can come for the ride, if you want, but it could be a long night."

"No, I'll go home," she said.

"Don't."

Now it was her turn to look at the clock. "There isn't even a late show on now."

"You can sleep. You can read. There are thirty-two hundred books in this place. You can listen to music."

"Or I could go home."

I started to dress.

"You don't really have to go, do you?" she said quietly.

"Ike Roth is my cousin. He's blood. A long time ago, when I was young, he was nice to me."

She leaned over and touched me.

"Go ahead out there. I'll stay."

I sat down on the edge of the bed and kissed her. She put a cool hand on the back of my neck and pressed me forward. Her thighs were smooth against my face.

"It won't take long," she said. "You promised."

The joints along Queens Boulevard were closing up, and a few of the hardcore drunks were lurching to the diners and the ritualized brawls that would end the evening. I took a right on Union Turnpike heading for Deepdene Road, looking for Ike's house. I had only been there twice before, years ago. Sarah was eight years older than Ike, and when they started having kids, we drifted apart. Sarah was one of those women who had waited a long time to be mothers and were determined to make the best of it; she had. The kids were grown now, a boy and a girl named Jason and Naomi, and the last time I had seen Sarah she was a nice, plump, jolly woman who liked her house and her women's clubs, and talked in great detail about education. It wasn't the way my life had turned out, so I didn't go there much. But I liked her. And I liked my cousin, Isaac Roth. I liked them a lot.

The house wasn't hard to find. Two lights, shaped like candles, flanked the white door. All the other houses were dark, their gabled rooftops soaked with rain. I found a parking spot a half block away and sprinted back and crossed the wet lawn. There was a brass knocker, and I rapped it twice.

Sarah answered the door. She was dressed in a flowery housecoat and floppy pink slippers and she seemed younger than I had remembered her. It had something to do with the blue-rinsed hair, and the pale ivory skin. She took my right hand in both of hers.

"Come in, Sam, quick. You'll catch a death of cold."

The first cop was planted against the wall inside the foyer. He was wearing a black raincoat and a gray hat and was holding an unlit cigar. His skin was dark and meaty, the color of rare roast beef, and someone had once rearranged his nose. His bleak, iron-colored eyes blinked in an odd rhythm.

"Who's this?" he said. The tone was perfect. The tone that says I'm a cop, I'm tough, I think everybody's guilty and I don't take any crap. The tone that always made me want to commit felonious assault on a police officer.

"Ike's cousin, Sam," Sarah said.

"What kind of cousin?" the cop said. He looked as hard as stone.

"Who are you?" I said.

"Somerville, Forty-seventh Squad," he said coldly, his mouth moving up and down like a trap door.

"Let's see your tin, Jack," I said.

He blinked in that out-of-synch way, pulled out a wallet, flashed a shield and started to put it away.

"Hold it, buster," I said. "I want to *see* it. I want to write down all the little numbers."

"I showed all I have to show, sport."

I took a pen and an index card out of my jacket pocket, held them in one hand, and opened the other hand flat.

"Let's see the tin, Somerville, or I'll put you out of here on your ass."

He pinched his bent nose. "Tough guy, huh?"

"Tougher than you, Blinky."

"I don't have to show you nothing."

I took out my wallet, slipped the press card out and held it in front of his face.

"Read this, Blinky. Now *you* know who *I* am. But you're a stranger in this house and I still don't know who *you* are. You might be a burglar, for all I know."

Somerville blinked, brushed the press card aside, and then showed me the badge again. I wrote down his badge number and made him tell me his name. James Somerville. A press card can't get you on the subway without some coin but it does mean you can call up a police commissioner and complain about the help.

"Thanks," I said. "Before we go any further, let me remind you of something. You work for me. I don't work for you. I pay the taxes that pay your salary, along with Sarah here and a few other citizens. You're a civil servant. That means you gotta serve, and you gotta be civil. Now, where's your partner?"

"In there," he said flatly, jerking a thumb in the direction of the living room.

"Thanks, Somerville."

Sarah followed me into the large living room. A beige rug covered the floor, with two chocolate-brown suede couches at right angles to the fire-place, and a green velour couch running the length of the front windows. There were muted lamps on end tables, and some good drawings on the wall, one of which looked like a Matisse. Framed photographs of Ike and Sarah and their kids stood on top of the grand piano, and on the mantelpiece. The place felt like a good home.

The other cop was sitting in the corner of one of the suede couches, his right foot on his left knee. He was small and red-haired and he smiled when we came in.

"You're Sam Briscoe, aren't you?" he said brightly.

"Yeah."

"I read you for years."

I could feel Somerville's bulky shape looming behind me.

"Relax, Jimmy. This is Sam Briscoe, you know, the newspaperman."

"I know," Somerville said. "He showed me his press card."

"You're a hell of a newspaperman," the second cop said. "You wrote great stuff from Vietnam."

"I'm a former newspaperman now."

"That's right," he said, feigning surprise. "I don't see the column in the paper anymore. How come you still have a press card?"

"I freelance. Sometimes it comes in handy."

"That's unusual, isn't it?" he said, without moving. "A freelancer with a press card?"

"Yeah, I guess it is. They must like me at headquarters."

"I'll have to ask them about that," he said, smiling. "Freelancers with press cards. That's unusual."

"There's the phone," I said. "You can get the commissioner at home, if it's bothering you."

He smiled again. "Ah, well, it's late. Anyway I'm Jerry Malone, homicide."

"What are you doing here, Malone?" I said.

Sarah fiddled with her hands. "I'll make some coffee, I think. You boys must be cold from that rain."

"Do you have tea, Sarah?" Malone said. "That caffeine is murder."

"Sure. Sam?"

"Tea's fine, Sarah."

Somerville grunted; he obviously wanted coffee. Sarah went through a door into the kitchen; I could see a lot of shiny dark brown appliances before the door swung shut. Malone stared at me. He was a shrewd, tough little bastard who had used the jab about the press card to tip me off balance. I waited for him to throw the right hand.

"How well did you know Ike Roth, Sam?" he said, lighting a Marlboro.

"He was my first cousin."

"I got first cousins I haven't seen in twenty years," he said. "Were you close?"

"We saw each other a lot when we were kids," I said. "He was older than me, but he was my best friend. Then he went in the Army, and when he was about to get out, I went in the Navy. So we didn't see much of each other for a long time. We saw each other for a while after I got discharged, but then I went to school in Mexico on the GI Bill and when I got back, Ike was married. So no, we didn't see much of each other. We talked on the phone."

"What about his kids?"

"What about them?"

"Did you see them much? Jason and . . . Naomi, right?"

"I didn't know them. They were kids. They're away now in school."

"So then you really haven't seen Ike for a long time."

"What are you driving at, Malone?" I said. "Why don't you just ask me?"

"You know what I'm driving at, Sam."

"I do?"

"You saw Ike Roth at the Garden tonight, Sam. He was with a cheap hoodlum named Carmelo Fischetti. And right there in the Garden tonight, with twenty thousand people around him, Carmelo Fischetti managed to get himself killed. You know that, Sam, because you took a look at the corpse."

That was the right hand. I lit a cigarette.

"Ike wouldn't kill anybody," I said quietly. "He isn't the type."

"Anybody can kill," Malone said. "There's no type."

He was right about that.

"Ike just isn't the type," I said, without conviction.

"Ike was in the diamond business, wasn't he?" Malone said.

"Yeah."

"Well?"

"Look at this place," I said. "It's nice, but it's not a mansion. If Ike was rich, he wasn't showing it off."

"Suppose he was trying to *get* rich?"

"His kids were grown. What would be the point?"

Behind me, I heard Somerville breathe out hard. He was leaning against the door frame leading to the foyer. Beside him, there was a drawing of a ballet dancer by Isaac Soyer.

"What's the matter, Somerville?" I said to him. "Smoking too much? Having trouble breathing?"

"Lay off him, Briscoe. He's a good cop."

Sarah came in carrying a tray. A ceramic teapot was flanked with cups, and she had put together a dish of lemons and a plate of Oreo cookies. The lemons gleamed against the white bone china of the plate and for some reason I thought of Marta and her Caribbean face, waiting for me in that part of the world that Ike and Sarah didn't know about. Somerville sat down on the couch across from me and reached for a cookie. He was still wearing his raincoat.

"Sarah," Malone said, "did Ike pack a bag for his trip to San Juan?"

"Why, yes. Of course. With extra shirts and everything. I packed for him myself. He said he might be gone a week."

"Do you know what flight he was on?"

"No, no, not really . . ."

"How would she know?" I said. "A guy going on a business trip doesn't give all the details."

"Let her answer, Briscoe," said Somerville, reaching for his third Oreo.

"I don't know what flight he was on," Sarah said quietly. "He'd been to San Juan three or four times in the last year. It was a night flight, though. He had time to eat dinner before leaving."

"Did he take a cab?" Malone said.

"No, he drove his own car. It's a wine-colored Mercury Cougar, this year's model."

"Was he carrying diamonds, Sarah?"

Her pale face grew even more pale. "I don't know. Would you mind telling me what this is all about?"

Malone stood up. "We're not absolutely sure yet, Mrs. Roth. Mind if we look around?"

She glanced at me and then at the stairs leading to the second floor. "Ike's not here."

"Oh, I know that," Malone said. "But we'd be pretty dumb if we didn't look."

"So look," she said sharply.

They moved through the two-story house, opening and closing doors, with Sarah behind them, her arms folded across her chest, like a woman whose house was being inspected for a summer rental.

I stayed in the living room, sipping the tea and looking at the pictures. There were photographs of Ike and Sarah getting married, standing with a beaming rabbi and Sarah's happy mother and pensive father. There was Ike in the Army, looking snappy outside Schofield Barracks in Pearl Harbor, with the palm trees in the background; Ike with Naomi and Jason at Jason's bar mitzvah; Ike and Sarah and Jason at a high school graduation; Sarah and Naomi at somebody's wedding; all of them together on the beach at Miami. There was even a picture of Ike with me. I was about fourteen, and he was seventeen, and we were both in boxing trunks at the old Loew Center PAL gym. I was only a lightweight then and Ike was a middleweight, and we both had a lot more hair. Next to it, there was a picture of Ike's father and my Grandmother Esther together, brother and sister off the boat from Europe, she already in her twenties and Ike's father about six. A piece of Ellis Island was in the background. So was the Statue of Liberty. Then Esther was with my grandfather, Jackie Briscoe, holding a baby. The baby was my father. Then it is the early thirties and Ike's father is standing with my father on some street in Brownsville. My father is about twenty, his hands held tightly to his side, his elbows tucked into his waist, his mouth a thin line, trying to look like Cagney in a tight-fitting suit, and managing to look like all the other young men from the corner of Georgia and Livonia who ended up in Murder Incorporated while he was studying for the cops' test. My mother isn't in any of the pictures. Kathleen Houlihan Briscoe was a shiksa, but that wasn't the reason. She just despised cameras. She came from the west of Ireland, and thought that cameras were thieves of the soul, and there had been times in my life when I thought she was right.* They were all dead now, and Ike Roth was in bad trouble.

I heard Somerville's heavy feet thumping down the carpeted stairs, and turned to see Malone coming down behind him, and Sarah last, her face clouded.

"Well, we'll be in touch," Malone said. Then to Sarah: "You're sure you don't know what's in the safe?"

"No, it's Ike's. We've had it for twenty years, and I've never looked in it once."

"We might have to open it," Malone said.

"You better see a judge first," I said.

"We will," he said in a tired voice.

Somerville angled around and picked up the last Oreo cookie.

"You got a home phone, Briscoe?" Malone said.

"Yeah," I said, and gave him the number that I always let the service pick up.

"Let me know if you hear from Ike," Malone said.

I nodded, and they went to the door and Sarah let them out. The rain had stopped. Somerville threw me a last murderous look.

5.

Sarah turned the little knob that locked the door, glanced at me, and rushed past me into the living room. She plunged onto the couch, grabbing a small cushion, and buried her face in it. Her body heaved with wracking sobs, like a young girl whose date had not shown up for the prom. I sat on the edge of the cocktail table, and touched her shoulder.

"Oh, Sam, oh, Sam, he's in trouble, Sam. I knew it. I knew, I knew. Oh, Sam. He's in terrible trouble and I knew. Poor Ike. Poor Ike. That poor sweet man."

I let her cry until there were no tears left. She lay still for a while and then lifted her face off the pillow and looked at me.

"What did you know, Sarah?" I said quietly.

She dried her face with her sleeve.

"I knew there was something going on. I knew by the way he was acting. The way he just went silent when I talked to him. I thought it was just because the youngest had gone off to college, Naomi, and he had to adjust. You know, to us being just two people, after always having someone else around too."

She sat up.

"But it wasn't that."

She went silent then, staring at her hands.

"What was it, Sarah?"

She looked at me squarely. "I don't really know. Maybe it was a woman."

"Why do you think that?"

"The hours he kept. Staying out late. Missing supper. Forgetting to call. It wasn't like him. Then staying out all night. Saying he couldn't get a cab. Or his car was broke down. Then not really saying anymore. He . . . We never . . . For more than a year, we . . . "

Her voice trailed off. The clock on the mantel said it was almost five. Traffic was beginning to move outside.

"Sometimes men go through change of life too," I said softly. "It could have been just a stage he had to go through."

"Maybe."

"What was his business like?"

"I never knew," she said, happy to change the subject. "He was one of the old-fashioned types. He kept a bank account for me, for household expenses, things like that. He was always generous, Sam. Anything I wanted I could have. Fur coats, an extra car. If I wanted them I could have them. He always said that. But I didn't want any of that. I wanted him, and the kids, and a nice home. That's all. That's all I ever wanted."

"Did you ever go to his office?"

"To the old office down on the Bowery near Canal," she said. "But I never went to the new office. He took a new partner, some Israeli with a heavy accent. Lev Pinchos, his name was, but I never met him." A pause. "They had an office on Forty-seventh Street, but she never invited me."

"That's the heart of the diamond business, that street."

"I know," she said. "About six months ago, I went over there with Jason. He had to get a book for some course at Harvard and the only store that had it was the Gotham Book Mart on Forty-seventh Street. We got the book and I thought, you know, that I should call Ike and come up and meet the new partner and see what the office was like. I called. But Ike said I shouldn't come up, he had some big customer up there, it was better if I didn't come up."

"He was probably telling the truth," I said lamely. "Those offices on Forty-seventh Street are mostly tiny little cubicles. I wrote a piece about the place once."

"It was his voice that was strange, Sam. You don't live with someone that long without knowing when something's wrong. That weekend was the first time he went to Puerto Rico. That Sunday night, Jason went back to school on the Boston shuttle and for the first time in years I was alone. I must have walked around this house for hours. He told me he was staying at the Hilton down there."

"The Caribe Hilton?"

"Right. So that Saturday night, I called down there. They rang the room and a woman answered, and I hung up. I was so ashamed. Ashamed of my own jealousy. Ashamed of being the typical wife. The aging wife. The wife getting traded in on a new model. The wife right out of some soap opera. And I was ashamed of going so far as I did to try to track him down. I told myself that I only wanted to talk to him, to cheer him up, to speak, you know, to the man I loved. To my husband. But it was worse than that, Sam. I *wanted* that woman to answer." A pause. "I wanted to know."

The tears started to well in her eyes again. I held her hand.

"And knowing that Ike had a woman down there made me feel superior," she said. "I had never slept with anyone but Ike. In all those years. In all my life. And I was still that way, and now he wasn't, and it made me feel better. When he came back, three days later, with his tan, I acted as if nothing had happened. That was my way of dealing with it. I made believe it had happened to someone else. Not to me. Not to Ike. And I could have gone along that way, except that he wouldn't talk to me. And then he went two more times to Puerto Rico, and I knew it wasn't just a weekend thing, a—a—what do they call it? A one-night stand?"

"Some people call it that."

"But now . . . What's going on, Sam? What's going to happen to us?"

"I'll try to find out," I said. "I promise you that."

"How much trouble is he in?"

"He could be involved in a murder," I said.

She moaned and turned her back and cried for another long while. I wished I could take the words back, but I couldn't. It was the second time I'd told her that, but now, at half-past five, after a long night, after telling me things she had probably never told anyone, after exposing her pain and her fears and her loneliness, murder must have sounded like something terribly final. She cried until she fell asleep.

I put out some of the lights and then went upstairs to see what the cops had seen. The master bedroom was large and warm, with a dark wooden headboard on the king-sized bed, muted lights on the night tables, a deep ochre spread and plump double pillows. I opened the closet, looking for a blanket. On the left were Sarah's clothes. The right side of the deep closet was half-empty. Ike had taken a lot of clothes with him. Maybe enough to stay away for good.

There was an extra blanket on a shelf and I brought it downstairs and covered Sarah. She was deep into a thick sleep. Then I went back to the second floor. Off the central corridor were the master bedroom, a bedroom for each of the kids, two bathrooms, and a den. I looked into the kids' rooms. They looked like kids' rooms everywhere: school pennants, funny animals, old baseball gloves, school pictures, shelves of books, some posters of rock stars and movie people. I went into the den.

Under the windowsill, there was a small, old-fashioned black iron safe, the kind you once saw in the offices of small businesses before everything went plastic and automated. I tried the door, but it was locked. I went to the desk. The top was almost clear, as if it had not been used very much. There were photographs of Sarah and the kids in group frames, and a blotter that had no sign of ink on it. I sat down and opened the drawers. In one drawer there were embossed letterheads for the firm of Pinchos and Roth in various sizes, with an address at 15 West 47th Street, and I folded one and slipped it into my jacket pocket. The main drawer was full of pencils, paperclips, rubber bands, felt pens, the usual miscellaneous clutter. The drawers on the left were empty, except for one folder of mail. An appeal from the UJA. A subscription offer from *People* magazine. A brochure selling *The Seafarers* from Time-Life Books. And a three-month-old thank-you note from something called the Greater Brooklyn Development Corporation. I folded that one and put it in my jacket. There wasn't anything else. Ike had either cleaned out the desk, or never really used it.

Across the room, past the door, there was a small three-shelf book case, but it didn't tell me very much. One shelf was stacked with technical books on the diamond and gem industry, along with a pile of old jewelry catalogues. There were some best-sellers on the next shelf, a few travel books about Europe and Asia, a Spanish dictionary. A conventional mix. I was opening one of the travel books when I froze.

I heard a click downstairs. The front door opened, then closed.

I put the book down and moved to the door and listened. It was quiet for a long time. Then someone was coming up the stairs, walking softly on the carpets. A board squeaked under weight. I could hear breathing. Each of the doors to the bedrooms was tried. I held my breath as he came closer to the den.

A man stepped in, and I chopped at his neck, and spun him, and threw the hook at his face. He was tall, bearded, his eyes masked by shades, dressed in black jacket and turtleneck. He fell hard against the desk and I moved on him and he

45

grunted and kicked at my belly, and whirled, swinging a heavy wrench. I bent under the arc of the swing and drove a punch to his balls. He groaned and dropped the wrench and stepped back and I knocked the glasses off with the next punch. One eye was blue, the other covered with a patch.

He cursed me, in another language.

And then my head split open, and I stood on a ledge above a deep and endless crevasse, tottering and unsteady, and then fell away into the darkness.

6.

I woke up beside the book case. The wrench was in my hand, and pain slithered in my head like a great thick worm trying to eat its way out of my skull. I let go of the wrench and tried to get up. My body wouldn't do what I told it to do. I could see a drawer lying on its side behind the desk, and *The Seafarers* brochure from Time-Life Books lying there, the envelope torn open. I got my arm to move and felt the top of my head and found the soft, pulpy mound where I'd been hit. There must have been two of them. Of course, schmuck. There are always two of them.

I saw lemon-colored light leaking through the venetian blinds. It was morning. Maybe. It could have been afternoon. I tried again to get up, and this time my body obeyed. The room was a shambles: torn books, an overturned book case, scattered drawers, papers, clips, pens. I stepped over the mess to the door. Bile rose in my stomach. I listened but heard nothing.

I went out into the hall, and everything had

been tossed, torn, ripped or opened. Everything. The tops were off the toilet tanks. Bedclothes had been torn from the beds, the mattresses slashed open. School pennants were gone from the walls. A catcher's mitt had been sliced open. The books were all over the floors, the hardcovers torn down their spines. They had gone through the house as methodically as an army patrol ransacking an enemy village.

"Sarah!" I shouted weakly.

There was no answer.

I walked to the top of the stairs and looked down. The main floor had also been invaded. The drapes were still drawn and two lamps were over on their sides, providing yellow bars of slanting light.

"Sarah!"

She didn't answer, and I started down, gripping the banister, nauseated by the pain, afraid I would fall. The carpets had been pulled up. All the pictures on the walls were now on the floor, their backings slashed open. I saw one lovely small magenta painting by Helen Frankenthaler with a jagged slice through its face. The piano was open, the stool lying on its side, all the photographs piled in disarray on the floor. The kitchen floor was covered with a mash of spilled food, open yogurt and cottage cheese cups, milk emptied from containers, frozen food chopped open, soap powders emptied on top of the wet slimy mess.

I went back into the living room. Dry ashes from the fireplace lay scattered on the rug. All the couches had been gutted, their stuffing lying in mounds. Beside the couch, in the half-darkness, was a crumpled thing wrapped in a green blanket. I went over and slowly pulled aside the blanket. The lumpy thing was red with blood. Its forehead was caved in. Some of its front teeth had been broken off. Its eyes were hidden behind the crimson mask.

The thing was Sarah.

The room moved, the floor tilting up at me, and I started to fall. I lurched to the side, and reached out, angling away for yards, then miles, until my hand found the fireplace. I braced myself and stood there for a long time not looking at the thing. The phone rang. I couldn't see it under the mess, but even if I had, I couldn't have answered it. I stared at the noise, listening to its muffled ring. It rang eleven times and then stopped. When it stopped, I found I could move again.

I went back upstairs, through the violated house, and stepped into the bathroom beside the den. Every jar, tube, and capsule had been opened, their pastes and powders dumped into the stoppered sink. I picked a towel off the floor and went into the den. The wrench was where it had fallen. I wiped it clean with the towel, except for the very end, which was furry with a small knob of blood and hair.

I carried the wrench to the stairs and dropped it into the living room. I threw the towel into the bathroom, and found a phone and called Somerville and Malone. For the first time I looked at my watch. It was almost 7:30. They had done all this in about two hours.

They're good, I thought.

They're really good.

Somerville and Malone arrived in a blue Plymouth. They came up the flagstone walkway and I was waiting there for them. Down the block, Red Emma was where I'd left her. Cars were pulling out of houses all along the street, bound for the offices of Manhattan. It had taken the cops fourteen minutes to get to the ruined house.

"Hello, big writer," Somerville said.

I didn't say anything.

"Where is it?" he said.

"She's in the living room," I said. "Beside the couch."

Malone squinted at me, searching my face, and they stepped past me together, Somerville leading the way. His big feet thumped on the hardwood floor of the foyer, and then stopped.

"Jesus Christ," Malone said softly.

Somerville whirled and slammed me against the wall.

"You son of a bitch."

"Easy, big boy," I said.

"The writer. The big fucking writer."

"I didn't write this," I said.

"Where you're going," he said, "you'll have lots of time to fucking write, scumbag."

Malone stepped between us, facing Somerville.

"You better make the usual calls," Malone said quietly. Somerville grunted and went into the kitchen. "Jesus Christ," I heard him mumble, as he dialed the first number. "Jesus fucking Christ."

Malone put his hands on his hips and looked around.

"What time did this happen?" he said.

"After you left, we talked maybe a half-hour," I said. "She fell asleep on the couch. I went upstairs, got a blanket for her, covered her, then went to see what Ike took with him when he left. Someone got in the house and cold-cocked me. I came around maybe an hour ago, maybe less. I didn't look at my watch. I could barely look at anything."

"What brought you over here anyway?"

"Sarah was worried about Ike, and so was I. When that thing happened in the Garden, I called her and told her that if she needed help, she could call me. She did."

He looked into my eyes, very carefully.

"You run a consolation service for relatives or something?" he said.

"Years ago, Ike was my best friend."

He looked back into the room.

"Was he in any kind of trouble?"

"I don't know," I lied.

He went over to the kitchen door, cracked it open and peered in at the floor. Somerville was still on the phone.

"Diamonds or dope," Malone said. "They were looking for something pretty small. Since your cousin Ike is in the diamond business, we oughta figure it's diamonds, right?"

"All I know is they were thorough," I said. "They even looked in my head."

Somerville came out of the kitchen and headed upstairs. I fingered the knot on my head. Malone reached over and touched it, looking at his fingers when he took his hand away. His fingertips were a pale red, but his face was as plain as dough.

"It's a good rap on the nut," he said.

"Yeah."

"Of course you could have done it to yourself."

"Sure," I said, "but maybe throwing myself out the window would have been more convincing. On the other hand, I might be trying to prove that I am one of the dumbest bastards on earth. If so, I played this perfect. I come over here, I talk to you and Somerville, I say goodnight, and then I right away commit a murder, and end the night by knocking myself out. Wonderful." I fumbled for a cigarette. "Dumb, but still kind of wonderful."

Malone smiled thinly, as Somerville came down the stairs, staring at the mess on the living-room floor. The big man took out a handkerchief and stepped through some couch stuffing and picked up the wrench.

"Here's the tool," Somerville said. He held the wrench out for Malone's inspection as if it were an offering. Malone looked at it, but didn't touch it. He glanced at me and shifted back to Somerville.

"You made all the calls?" Malone said.

"They're all on the way," Somerville said.

"You tell anyone the Briscoe angle?"

"No."

"I don't have an angle," I said.

"Everybody's got an angle," Malone said.

"I never mentioned this scumbag," Somerville said. "I'm a civil servant. I was fucking civil. I was a fucking servant."

Malone glanced at me again, and at the wrench, and pulled at his lower lip. He walked into the living room. A fetid, fudgy smell of drying blood and loosened bowels stained the air.

"This cousin of yours," Malone said. "You don't know where he is?"

"I haven't a clue."

He looked at the thing beside the couch, and then at the demolished room.

"What about the safe?" he said to Somerville.

"It's gone."

"It's gone?"

"Unless they hid it pretty good or this bird shoved it up his ass," Somerville said, "it's gone."

Malone glanced up the stairs, and then at the door, as if tracing the route the lost safe had taken.

"It was still there when they slugged me," I said.

"What do you mean, 'they'?"

"There had to be more than one to carry that thing," I said. "It wasn't very big, but it was old and heavy."

Somerville walked around me, pausing, looking me over, as if getting ready to beat the truth out of me.

"You could have helped take it out of here," he said.

I moved with him as he circled me, and then stood as close to him as possible, calling on whatever will I had left.

"Listen, Somerville," I said, "why don't you just clerk this crime, make your notes, fill out your forms, and keep your fucking theories to yourself?"

His eyes shot to Malone for permission to destroy me, but I walked away, turning my back on him. I waited for the blackjack but it never came. If it had, my brain would have surrendered for good. Instead there was a quick, insistent knock at the door.

"Get that," Malone said, and Somerville lumbered to the door, and let in two ambulance attendants and a young Indian from India who must have been an intern. Somerville left the door open and a couple of young uniformed cops appeared, and he talked quietly to them, and they went back outside. Then a police photographer showed up, and a plainclothesman with a badge pinned to a tweed jacket, carrying a briefcase, who must have been the fingerprint man, and then someone from the M.E.'s office. And I sat on a clear section of the floor, letting the worm of pain finish eating my brain, while Malone looked me over and Somerville acted as tour guide for the new arrivals. I knew what they would do, because as a reporter I'd seen them do it in a lot of other places. They would examine her broken face and head; they would eventually lift her onto a stretcher; they would telephone her children; they would dust everything for the whorls and loops and ridges and tents of fingerprints and then they would try to find the people who did it to her. And I knew sitting there that I would have to try to find those people too. I would have to find Ike Roth. And then I would have to find those other bastards and hurt them a little harder than they'd hurt me, and maybe as hard as they'd hurt Sarah. I wasn't a cop, but this was family. This was about a nice woman and her once nice husband, and I would have to do something about it or I would never feel good again.

Malone moved around, his hands in his pockets, stealing glances at me, and finally he stood over me, with his hands in his trouser pockets and his raincoat bunched out behind him. He breathed out hard and took his hands out of his pockets.

"You might as well go," he said. "The D.A. can get a statement from you later."

He offered me a hand and I took it and got up slowly. "All right."

"You better get that head looked at," he said.

"Yeah."

He looked around the room again, where all the clerks of the city's violence were working at their tasks.

"I never get used to it," he said quietly. "I've seen them stabbed, poisoned, strangled and shot. I've seen them chopped up with meat cleavers and sliced open with bread knives. I never get used to it."

I saw one of Sarah's floppy pink slippers under a mound of gray ashes beside the fireplace.

"Who the hell does?" I said.

"Get going," he said.

"Thanks, Malone," I said.

"Don't thank me," he said. "I wish the fuck I'd never met you."

7.

Trouble always draws a crowd, and the patrol cars and the ambulance and the camera flashes from inside the house had drawn them all right: kids with schoolbooks under their arms, housewives with their hair in curlers, executives who didn't have to get to the office on time. They were all standing in the bright sunlight, lined up on the sidewalk across the street like movie extras waiting for commands from a director. Something terrible had happened. They knew that. And the details didn't matter. So they would wait for the crews from the TV stations and they would give properly shocked interviews and a few of them would cry on cue and later, at dinnertime, people all over the city would watch all of this on their Sonys and Admirals and Zeniths, and talk about how the city was becoming a jungle, and in two days, Sarah Roth, whose death had entertained them for five or six minutes, would be forgotten.

"What happened, mister?" said a freckled, red-haired kid in a tan poplin jacket.

"Something bad," I said, turning right at the end of the flagstone path, and walking down the street to the car.

"Real bad?" he said eagerly.

"Real bad."

"Is someone dead?"

"Someone's dead."

"Murdered?"

I opened the door with my key. "Why don't you go to school, kid?" I said. "It'll all be on TV tonight."

"Yeah?"

Yeah, it would be on television, all right, and splashed across the front pages of the newspapers, and as I pulled out, I thought of all the places I had been sent to when I was a kid reporter, to stand in the rain waiting for the cops to tell me what had happened; places where bodies lay on the kitchen floor, and Marlboro packs floated in the blood; places where little girls had been raped and thrown off rooftops; places where marriages had ended in the most final of divorces with a sash-weight delivering the decree, and no alimony later; and I was glad I didn't work on a newspaper anymore, didn't have to become a paid tourist in other people's tragedies. But this was different; this was family; and nobody was going to pay me for covering it. But somebody was going to pay.

I drove down Queens Boulevard, the car purring and light and easy to the touch. I looked behind me and saw no cops in the choked morning traffic. I pulled over in front of a saloon called Gallaghers, thinking about Sarah, wondering whether she had pleaded with them before they had clubbed her into eternity, wondering who was going to tell her kids. It would have to be the cops. It sure wasn't going to be me. The streets were gleaming in the sun, rain-washed and sparkling, with a cool breeze blowing from the river. I went inside. Two men with rum-hurt faces were nursing morning beers at the bar. I went past them to the pay phone and called Marta. On the fourth ring, she picked up.

"Hullo," she said thickly.

"It's me," I said.

"What time is it?"

"Almost eleven."

"*Coño carajo,*" she said.

"I'm sorry I never got back there. I'm still in Queens."

"Jesus, Sam, what—"

"I need some help. Do you have to work today?"

"I told them yesterday that I wouldn't be in. Did you get any sleep?"

"No, Ike's wife was murdered last night."

"*What?*"

I told her what had happened. She made a small swallowing sound. Where she came from, violent death wasn't so unusual; but it wasn't like playing a number either.

"They *beat* her to death?"

"With a lug wrench, I think. The cops think so too."

"Oh, wow."

"And I want to get those bastards."

I heard her lighting a cigarette. "What can I do to help, Sam?"

"Just one thing. Find that blonde."

"Ileana."

"Yeah. Get a last name for her," I said. "And an address. But don't get directly involved. Don't get brave. Call me. I'm heading home now to try to sleep a few hours. Don't wait for me."

"I'll try to find her, Sam."

"The cops don't know about her," I said. "But these other people might. So be careful. All I want is a name and an address."

"All right," she said. "Are you okay?"

"My head hurts, and I'm so tired my bones are melting, and I don't smell too good. Otherwise, I'm fine."

"I'll call you later."

Chuck Simpson was blowsy with sleep when I knocked at his door on Bank Street. Once, years ago, he had been the highest-paid abortionist in New York, with a clientele that included most of the gilded children of the upper East Side. But he had been caught on a tip from a jealous husband, his picture was published in the paper, the judge knew the jealous husband, and he had been jailed and disbarred. The medical societies never gave him back his license, and so he tended bar around the Village and handled a few neighborhood emergencies and listened to a lot of music and complained that he was like all those Catholics who were frying through eternity in hell for eating meat on Fridays during the centuries before Pope John changed the rules. He ran his long, tapered fingers through his gray hair.

"What is it this time, Sam? The clap or the gout?"

"The head."

He closed the door behind me and touched my head tenderly.

"Beautiful," he said. "Another friendly neighborhood husband?"

"Just clean it, Chuck. I can hardly talk, never mind explain."

I sat in a reclining chair, feeling the rush of nausea move through me again. Chuck opened a cabinet behind me. I heard glass on wood. I heard him wash his hands. I heard music from another room, a flute playing something elegant and haunting. Mozart.

"That's beautiful," I said. "The flute."

"It's this kid James Galway. Irish kid. Better than Rampal. Better than anybody."

He cut away some of my hair, and swabbed the wound with cotton and disinfectant. My scalp burned, then tingled and I enjoyed the feeling. The stinging pain was at least definitive, not murky like nausea.

"I'd love to hear him play with Miles," Chuck Simpson said.

"I'd like to hear anyone play with Miles."

"Even Harry Truman?"

"Even Truman Capote."

He put another fluid on the damaged skin, and then a bandage. His moves were quick and steady and professional.

"You really should get an EEG," he said. "Want me to call someone?"

"I don't have time. It's not broken, is it?"

"No, but I don't know about the brain. You seem to have a good, thick Irish skull. But the brain is

60

tender. Like a yolk in an eggshell. Whack it around and you can ruin it."

"I'll come back when I have time, Chuck."

I got up and slipped him a twenty, which he took without words. "Listen, with the new governor, you think there's any chance of a pardon for me, Sam?"

"Maybe. I'll drop him a note and tell him not to do it. You go back to work legit, and I lose a cut man."

"You really oughtta get an EEG. Your brain's like oatmeal." He lit a cigarette. "I can tell from the way you talk."

Marta was gone when I got back to the loft. I went into the shower, pulled a shower cap over the bandage and let the hot needled water beat at me for a long time. I sat down and dried myself. Then I started up the ladder to the sleeping bay. For a moment, I thought I wouldn't make it. The room began to swim and a warm, sickly sweetness leaked from the back of my throat and the edges of the long room pushed up at me. I was sure I would fall and hit my wounded head and my brain would just sigh in protest and collapse and I would be dead. Just like that. After all the wildness of my life I would die in an eight-foot fall, and thinking that, I felt silly and sick and legless, holding on tightly while my hands seemed to fill with water. Each finger was just a tube, filling up, without bone or tendon or muscle. I hooked my chin onto one of the wooden rungs in the ladder and did not move.

And then the room stopped spinning, and the

water seeped out of my hands, and one of my legs
returned to life and the warm, sickly sweetness
passed. I could move again. I climbed the last
few rungs and dragged myself over to the bed.
Marta had smoothed the sheets and covers and
cleaned the ashtrays before she left, and I thought:
I could marry a girl like that. And thought right
after that: you like her too much to make her suffer
that way. And then tried to think one more thing,
which wouldn't come, before falling away into
sleep.

8.

    I dreamed of a long dark tunnel with wet, obsidian walls and old men with heavy black beards and thick, hairy, many-fingered hands waiting in the distance. My father stood over on the side, his eyes staring, his arms folded across his chest the way he always folded them when he was being stern. He said nothing, and I moved past him, deeper into the tunnel. The tunnel curved away into a darker place, with the sound of water dripping, and then the bearded men were chasing me and I came into a large dark cavern with stalactites hanging from the ceiling and an underground river flowing off to the right, disappearing into fog. I was filled with dread. And Ike Roth was in a boat, drifting on the ragged edge of the fog, calling my name and waving. He had all of his hair and was wearing corduroy pants and was about twelve years old. The boat drifted into the fog and the bearded men were after me again and I started to call for my father, screaming his name in the echoing darkness, plead-

ing with him to save me, knowing he would
not come, and then the men were on me.

And I was awake.

Sweating, drained, exhausted.

It was gray and dark in the loft now, and I lay
still for a long while, trying to push away the
dream with the reality of the night before, each
terrible fragment coming forth to present itself
to me like an actor at an audition. My body
ached. My head was sore. I went into the shower
again, and shaved under the nozzle, and got
dressed.

The story was on the 4:30 news on WINS, telling
about the brutal killing of Sarah Roth in those
clipped terse sentences that sound so flat and allow
the commercials to sound so lively. The announcer
talked about how police were attempting to find
the husband of the slain woman, and how he was
believed to be in Puerto Rico on a business trip.
The voice said that intruders had apparently broken
into the Roth home in Forest Hills, ransacked the
apartment and bludgeoned the woman to death.
A small safe had been taken from the Roth den,
and found near LaGuardia Airport with its door
blown off and empty. The Roth children had
arrived home from college that afternoon but had
declined to speak to reporters. Something in the
announcer's tone made you think that the children
were the prime suspects because they would not
provide the conventional New-York-is-a-jungle interviews in twenty-five words or less to the people
with the mikes. It didn't matter, because the neigh-
bors had given the microphones what they wanted.
One neighbor even blamed the welfare people from
a housing project, fourteen blocks away. I listened

carefully but the announcer did not mention Ileana, and did not connect the death of Sarah Roth to the death in Madison Square Garden the night before. He did not mention me.

The phone rang.

"Hello, handsome," Marta said.

"Where are you?"

"My place."

"Any luck?"

"Maybe."

"What's that mean?"

"It's complicated. I don't want to talk on the phone," she said. "But it can hold. Where should I meet you?"

"Don't go anywhere," I said. "I have a stop to make first, and I'll meet you at your place right after."

"How you feeling?"

"Horrible."

"Well that's better than dead."

"I'll see you later," I said and hung up.

I unfolded the letterhead of Pinchos and Roth, with its West 47th Street address, and dialed their number.

"Hello?" a voice said tentatively.

"Mr. Pinchos, this is Ike's cousin. Sam Briscoe."

He sighed. "Such a tragedy."

"I'd like to see you," I said. "I need to know a few things."

"I haven't heard from Mr. Roth in two days," he said quickly in a vaguely eastern European accent.

"I didn't think you had," I said. "But I need to talk to you."

"I told the police everything I know," he said.

"Yeah, and God works in a gay bath house."

"There just isn't much to say," he blurted. "Is there?"

"I'm afraid there is," I said. "Can you wait there for me?"

"I have several ap—"

"Wait there," I said. "I know some things that the police don't know. And so do you."

It was a shot in the dark. I had no idea what he knew. There was a long beat of silence.

"All right," he said. "I'll wait. Please hurry."

I hung up and called Charlie Kelly at Manhattan South Homicide to find out what he had on the Fischetti killing. He was out somewhere, and I left a number for him to call. I finished dressing, found an old porkpie hat in a closet, put it on over the bandage, pressed the button for the freight elevator and eased Red Emma out of my living room and into the elevator. The door locked behind me, and I pressed the button for the street level. Pepe, the guard, nodded hello as I pulled out and headed east for the Post. I parked under the FDR Drive, and crossed South Street to the main entrance.

"Well, Mr. Briscoe," the Pinkerton said.

"Hello, Wilbur. How's the kids?"

"My boy's gonna graduate next June," he said.

"That's great."

"I hope you're coming back to the paper," he said quietly.

"No, Wilbur, it's not my racket anymore."

His voice got conspiratorial. "We sure could use you around here."

"I'm just a visitor now. Is Mr. Matofsky in?"

66

"Hasn't left yet. You know the way, right?"

"I'll never forget the way, Wilbur."

I went up to the third floor in the elevator, the way I had gone so many times to the city room in the last years at the paper. When I started the paper was over on West Street, in a filthy little city room that opened onto the United Fruit Company docks, and in the summer the fruit flies would arrive in clouds, and we would type and smack, type and smack. I would write all night then, story after story, going out into the great, dark, exciting city, knocking on doors, looking at the living and the dead, and then head back and get it all into seven hundred words or less, and when that was done I would work the phones on other stories, or write picture captions, or go out again as dawn streaked the sky. The place was dirty and they didn't pay the talent and there was never enough staff. But I was young there and happy, and when they moved at last, to this shiny new city room on the other side of town, I never was comfortable again; I felt as if I needed a Blue Cross card to get in, instead of a press card.

The city room still looked like a hospital ward, with blue fluorescent lights tucked discreetly into the lowered ceiling and sweepers moving through the rows of desks, abandoned now by the day side, sweeping up the debris of a busy afternoon. Harvey Matofsky was reading wire copy at the city desk and he looked up when he saw me come in.

"We don't need anyone," he said, looking back at the wire copy. "Try the *News*. The *Bergen Evening Record*. Or if you're hard-up, the *Times*."

"I can't write stories that end with a recipe," I said.

"Then you better get out of the business," he said.

"Just give me a chance, sir. Just put me on the desk. Let me handle ship news. Give me weather and the horoscope. I've changed. I swear. No more drinking. No more throwing typewriters out the window. I'm in AA, with Richard Burton and Jason Robards. I've even found . . . God."

"Where was he? Up your ass?"

"No, sir. He was up yours, sir."

He spiked the copy, and tried to smile.

"What can I do for you, stranger?"

"First, fix your lip. You smiled. It's bleeding hard."

"It's all right, I got a chapstick in the car."

"I need some clips," I said.

He fumbled in the desk and came out with a brass key. A piece of adhesive tape on the round part said "Library."

"Help yourself," he said. "There's nobody back there. The new regime doesn't staff people around here much anymore."

"As compared to the old days?"

"Yeah, when Alexander Hamilton was the editor."

I hefted the key. "Thanks, Harve."

The library smelled of old paper and the past. The clips were in row after row of small brown envelopes, cross-indexed by name, subject matter, or by-line, and the place had been run masterfully for years by a guy named Pete Dinella. It always gave me a strange feeling being in there alone. My own past was there, but so was that of Cannon and Pegler and Ruark and Broun; passions of the day, great issues, small stories, tours in other people's tragedies, laughter, wit, lies and heartbreak: all were folded neatly into those three-by-five envelopes, and shoved into those drawers, where they would eventually get yellow and brittle and turn to dust. By tomorrow, there would be an envelope on Sarah Roth, with a handful of stories, and the word "dead" stamped on the front.

I moved fast. There were a few clips on Ike: accepting an award from the United Jewish Appeal, making a speech to the Jewelers Association, joining a group of fifty businessmen on a street sweep organized by the Association for a Better New York. He was in another clipping with his son, Jason, at the finals of the National Spelling Bee when the boy was eight years old and had finished third. The clip was from the old *World Telegram*. That was dead too. I put all the clips back in the wire basket for re-filing, found nothing on Pinchos, but grabbed everything I could find on Forty-Seventh Street, the diamond industry and Carmēlo Fischetti, stuffed them into my pockets, put out the lights and left. Pete Dinella would have had heartburn if he'd known I was taking clips out of the building; but Pete wasn't there anymore, and when I was finished I would send them back in the mail.

I walked down the hall to the elevator. Harvey Matofsky was at the water fountain.

"Hey, thanks for that tip last night," he said. "We got a dandy photograph of the late Carmelo Fischetti."

"The permanently late Carmelo Fischetti."

"He actually wasn't much of a hoodlum," he said. "It wasn't like getting Meyer Lansky with one in the breastbone. But the picture really worked."

A copy boy came off the elevator with a pile

of final editions, and Harvey took two, handing one of them to me. The picture of Carmelo Caggiano had lasted for all four editions, but Sarah Roth was the headline: INTRUDERS SLAY QUEENS HOUSEWIFE. There was a picture on the inside of Ike and Sarah with the kids: one of the pictures that had been swept off the piano, and probably slipped to the papers by the cops. In his page-one photograph, Fischetti was still sitting in his chair, with his head tilted back, and that stain on his chest.

"Did you get much on this bum?" I said, tapping Fischetti's chest.

"The usual. He had the usual wife, Rose something, who thought he was in the usual fruit and vegetable business. She showed our reporter the books of Green Stamps he would collect on his rounds. 'He would sit,' she said, 'and I would put.' They had the usual couple of daughters, who were under house arrest in the usual Catholic boarding school in Jersey. Let's see, what else? Oh, yeah. Our man Carmelo also had the usual yellow sheet from age thirteen, mostly assaults and robberies. He did a long bit in Greenhaven for manslaughter, and went to graduate school in Sing Sing. But there's nothing for the last ten years. The cops think he's been working with the Cubans in coke, shylocking and fencing, out in Brooklyn. You rip a diamond ring off an old lady, Carmelo'd turn it into a twenty-dollar bag. He goes back and forth a lot, from New York to Miami to San Juan. The usual middle-level executive in America's most successful corporation."

"Well, thanks, Harve."

"It's that one over in Forest Hills that's got the cops wiggy. They can't make that one out at all."

"I can imagine."

I went back to Red Emma and drove up South Street to the East River Drive. It was dark now and the traffic was heavy. The road was lumpy with potholes and loose gravel from badly laid asphalt rattled in the tire guards. Over to the right, lights were blinking on in Queens and Brooklyn and bars of red neon shimmered across the black waters of the East River from the Pepsi sign. I turned on the radio and the WINS announcer was reading the same stories he had read two hours earlier. I switched to FM and WRVR and listened to Stanley Turrentine play "Pieces of Dreams" while the traffic slowed and engines idled and Red Emma jerked and protested, demanding freedom, like a bird in a closet.

I pulled off the drive at Forty-second Street and inched up First Avenue through the evening rush hour. Buses and cabs warred with each other for space, and then an ambulance pulled into Forty-seventh Street, its siren screaming, trying to force passage, and I pulled in behind it. All horns were hit at once and I couldn't hear the radio anymore as the front line of cars at last ran the red light at Lexington Avenue and the ambulance pushed through behind them. I could see a man lying on his back on a stretcher. A purple tie hung loose at his throat, pointing to the floor, like an arrow of defeat. His face was the color of looseleaf paper, and he lay there helpless, dying of traffic.

I put the car in a Kinney lot near Sixth Avenue and walked back along Forty-seventh Street to the

building where Pinchos and Roth had their office.
I went past the Gotham Book Mart, where Ezra
Pound's *ABC of Reading* was standing beside Jim
Harrison's *Farmer*. Harrison was one of the best
writers in America, but nobody knew his name.
They knew Pound all right, but he was dead now,
and they knew him for all the wrong reasons, for
his lunacy and not his extraordinary talents in the
years when he was young. I was thinking about
both of them when I reached 15 West 47th Street.

The lobby was small, almost nondescript, with
a directory of names made of those little plastic
letters that are shoved into black felt. Pinchos and
Roth were in 1108. I pushed the button of the
small elevator. When it came down, a group of
Hasidim hurried out, most of them young, a few
bearded, all talking Yiddish. They were dressed
in black, wearing fur hats and side curls and as I
went into the elevator, a part of my afternoon
dream moved through me like a memory of winter.

9.

   The elevator opened into a four-foot-square cage. The cage ran from floor to ceiling and beyond it I could see a designing board, a battered desk, a few chairs. The office was shaped like an L, and most of it seemed to be around the corner of the L. The air was stale and close. I rang a buzzer and waited, remembering some old article I had written about how the gem business was a $4-billion-a-year racket and that half the deals were made right here on Forty-seventh Street, between Fifth and Sixth Avenues. That was ten years ago and now diamonds were bigger than ever, as the rich of France and Italy and the Middle East converted their fortunes into objects that could be carried away easily, a few steps ahead of the Communists. The stock market was shot, the dollar was falling, inflation got worse; but diamonds were forever. I pushed the buzzer again.

   "Hello," I said. "I'm here. Briscoe."

   Lev Pinchos shuffled around from the side of the L. He was very large, broad-shouldered, large-bellied, with rounded black shoes that would have been too big for Primo Carnera. He was wearing a black suit that stretched and pulled across his vast bulk, a white shirt buttoned to the top, no tie, white socks, and thick, highly polished glasses. I couldn't see his eyes behind the glasses. His skin was very white, almost pasty, the skin of an ex-convict. He too was wearing *payess*, or side curls, and a few lone strands of black hair decorated his skull. He was a Hasid, all right. He walked to within a yard of the cage, his giant feet dragging along slowly as if in sullen protest against the great weight they had to carry. He wheezed before he talked.

"Forgive me, sir," he said, the accent less pronounced than it was on the phone. "But I must see some identification."

"Of course," I said, and took out my wallet and showed him my press card. He stepped closer, and peered at the card through his glasses.

"A reporter?" he said cautiously.

"Yes. But I'm here as a relative, not as a reporter. I want to help find Ike."

He stared at me for a moment, then took a ring of keys from his pocket. He opened three locks and swung the cage door in, nodding welcome, and then closed it and locked all three locks again. He smelled vaguely of onions.

"Come in," he said, and led me to the other angle of the L, out of sight of the entrance. There was a long table covered with cutting, grinding and polishing wheels, engraving tools, a jeweler's bench. An oxygen torch was against one wall, under a calendar from the Central Luncheonette, and I saw a hot box and a small steamer for cleaning gems. A cheap reclining chair stood beside a barred window, which opened into an air shaft. A dented green four-drawer file cabinet had been shoved into a corner. There were a few pictures on the wall. One was of Ike Roth, standing beside a rabbi with an unkempt graying beard and steady intelligent eyes. Another was of Lev Pinchos. You had to look hard to recognize him. The big frame was there and the feet, but none of the meat. He was in a uniform and vertical stripes, standing alone behind grids of barbed wire.

"You were in one of the camps?" I said.

"Yes."

"Good God," I said.

"I survived," he said, glancing at the photograph, and then letting his eyes wander.

"Where were you?"

"Auschwitz," he said, with a wheeze. "I often wish it had been somewhere else. Auschwitz has become such a cliché, hasn't it? But that's where I was."

"Shtarbt men in der yungt iz es oyf der elter vi gefunen," I said in Yiddish. Dying while young is a boon in old age.

"Perhaps," he said sadly.

"You've put on some weight in your old age," I said.

"In my old age, I ate," he said. "I never got over the hunger. I have eaten fields of vegetables. I have eaten herds of cattle. They were never enough." He glanced back at the photograph. "I keep the picture as a reminder," he said, "and perhaps, as an excuse." He sighed in a phlegmy way. "Well, what can I do for you?"

"Where's Ike?" I said flatly.

He smiled. "That's what the police asked me, and I must give you the same answer I gave them. I don't know."

"He's your partner, isn't he?"

"Yes," he said. "We have been partners for more than a year."

"How did that work?"

"The partnership? I know gems. He knows people. So I did much of the inside work and Ike worked on the customers."

"When did you last see him?"

"Two days ago. Before he left for Puerto Rico."

He sat down on the recliner, his hands folded on his lap. The chair sagged.

"Why did he go to Puerto Rico, Pinchos?"

"To see a customer," he said. "A big customer. Ike had sold this customer things before. He had bought smaller items, and some bulk commercial diamonds. He must have come to trust Ike on the quality of the goods."

Pinchos shifted, squirmed, and got up. His right hand went to the right pocket of the jacket, where he began fingering what must have been a gun. Tiny beads of sweat pimpled his brow and upper lip and he swiped at them with the sleeve of his jacket. He stood very still, full of unsaid things, as if trying to decide something.

"We were new, but we had a certain reputation," he said hesitantly. "I have been on this street for five years. I have worked for many of the dealers. Ike knew more than I did. They trusted us. And this business is built on trust."

The words were reasonable and clear, but his voice was beginning to betray him. Something blurry, indefinite, hesitant was working in him now,

76

like an underground river. He put his hand into the pocket again, and quickly withdrew it, as if realizing immediately that the gun would provide him no solace. He seemed about to cry.

"All right," I said, "now tell me the real story."

He turned quickly, an alert, hard, thin man moving inside the prison of fat. When I talked tough, something in him smelled the gas.

"What do you mean, the real story?"

"The part you didn't tell the cops."

"I told the cops everything I knew," he said.

"Nobody ever tells the cops everything he knows."

"You're calling me a liar," he snapped.

"No, I'm not," I said. "I'm saying that you know a hell of a lot more than you're telling me."

Suddenly he whipped out the gun and pointed it at me. It was a police .38 with a dull blue-metal sheen. His hand was trembling. I wished I could see his eyes.

"Put that thing away, Pinchos."

"Now I want you to tell me what you know," he said. "I'm not afraid of killing you."

"That would be boring," I said, thinking that if you had survived Auschwitz, killing someone would be easy.

"I can shoot you, tell the police that you came here to rob me and nobody will doubt me. It happens all the time on Forty-seventh Street."

"Then why talk? Do it."

"I want to know . . ."

"If you don't put that fucking gun down I'll make you eat it."

For a moment he looked at the gun through the thick glasses, and I moved. I slapped his glasses away and grabbed the gun hand with both of mine. He shoved forward with the great weight, driving me hard across the office, and slammed me into the cage, rattling the steel frames. He tried to get his free hand to my throat, but I slipped down and away, for better leverage, and braced myself. I was still gripping the gun hand, which was at an odd angle over my left shoulder, and then he grabbed my hair, pulling my head back into line with the gun.

I kneed him hard in the balls, and he groaned, and then the gun went off. The noise was enormous, caroming off the walls of the L-shaped office, and Pinchos stepped back, his eyes spinning blindly. I jerked the gun hand down, driving my thumbs between his first and second knuckles, trying to split his hand.

His fingers loosened. I twisted my body, whipped around and smashed an elbow to his jaw. The gun clattered to the floor.

I stepped back and hit him once more on the chin. His legs went and the huge body skittered backwards, smashing into the jeweler's bench. The bench went over, the pans of the scale falling to the floor under him, as his big feet went up in the air.

"You stupid bastard," I said.

I stepped across him and went over and picked up the gun. He moaned and flopped clumsily on his side and tried to get up. I put the gun in my jacket pocket and then grabbed his hand. His eyes were small and blue, blinking in a wide, unfocussed way.

"Get up, putz," I said.

"*Momsa!*" he said, but didn't refuse my hand.

78

When he was standing, I looked around and found his glasses and handed them to him. They weren't broken. He slipped them on.

"You must have a brain the size of a diamond," I said. "One of us could have been killed just now. For nothing."

"Yes," he said softly.

"Sit down."

He went back to the reclining chair, his large body softer now than it had been a few minutes earlier. He flexed and unflexed the jammed knuckles of the gun hand.

"You might as well tell me the rest of it," I said.

"I don't have to tell you anything."

"Maybe not. But think for a moment. I have the gun now. Now I can shoot you with it. I can shoot you a little at a time. If nobody heard that first shot, they won't hear the next five either. They won't hear the shot that takes your elbow off. Or the one that ruins your knee. They won't hear the last one in your heart either."

I hefted the gun, and kept talking: "On the other hand, Ike's my cousin. If he's committed a crime, I'm not going to tell the cops. I know him. I know his moves. I know the way he thinks. If anyone can find him, I can. If he's alive, that is." I looked down the barrel of the gun, right at Pinchos' nose. "But if I have to go and find him, you've got to tell me everything. Not what you told the cops. The real story."

He sat there, making a small, solemn tent with his hands. Then he breathed out hard. I slipped the gun back into my pocket.

"Why not?" he said. "I'm ruined anyway. If Ike ever comes back, we'll be responsible for all of it.

The death of Ike's wife. And the other thing. The terrible thing."

"What other thing?"

He looked at his gun hand, still flexing the fingers, then turned it over and looked at his fingernails.

"The breastplate of Aaron," he said.

"The what?"

He smiled bleakly at me, and got up and went over to the file cabinet, opened a drawer and riffled through some folders. He took out a sheet of 35-millimeter slides and handed it to me.

"Look," he said.

I held the sheet up to the light and saw a number of photographs of the same extraordinary piece of jewelry. In this single piece there were twelve different rectangular stones, three across and four down, enclosed in a larger rectangle of gold. Two heavy gold hooks, looking like the braided candles of Passover, were attached to the corners. The piece was obviously designed to be worn with a chain around the neck. The colors of the gems were deep and luxurious, greens and reds and purples, something in amber, another black and burnished that must have been onyx, all of them glowing mysteriously, as if speaking across the centuries. On each stone a single word was engraved in Hebrew.

"This is the breastplate worn by Aaron, the first rabbi of the temple in Jerusalem," he said, in a hushed voice.

"Forgive me," I said, "I'm not much of a Jew. When was that, anyway?"

"Thirteen centuries before Jesus," he said.

It was my turn to speak in a hushed voice. I tapped the slide. "And this belonged to Aaron?"

"Every conceivable test indicates that it is the long-lost breastplate described in detail in the Book of Exodus. It was lost when the Babylonians took the Jews into captivity, but there were reports from time to time that it still existed."

His voice shifted into the clipped tones of an expert. "The lettering on each stone represents the names of each of the twelve tribes of Israel. For many centuries, the existence of the piece was seldom more than a rumor. It was reported in Rome, in Constantinople, in Persia. At the time of Justinian, it turned up in Jerusalem in the possession of a very brutal Roman general. But after the seventh century, it was not heard of again."

"Until now."

"Until now."

He leaned back in the recliner, staring at the blank ceiling. The blankness seemed to calm him. I looked at the photographs again and felt an odd sensation of relief, as if nothing happening right now could mean much when compared to the immensity of the dead centuries.

"It's beautiful," I said.

"Beautiful is so . . . small a word," he said. "Unbelievable, maybe . . ."

"And Ike had this with him . . . ?"

"Yes."

"How did you get your hands on it?"

He sat up in the recliner. "I can't tell you that."

"Why not?"

He sat there, staring at the sheet of slides, his face looking like a collapsed lung.

"I . . . I just can't say."

I knew that eventually he would, but I didn't press him.

"Well, at least give me some of the other facts," I said. "Like the name of the guy Ike was supposed to meet in San Juan."

"I didn't tell the police. Why should I tell you?"

"Because I can find him, that's why."

He got up and went to the battered desk, slid out a drawer and removed a flat gold case. He lifted a brown-papered Turkish cigarette, fingering it delicately, and lit it. He didn't offer me one.

"His name was Perez."

Curtains began to part in my mind.

"Monon Perez?"

"All I know is Perez."

"There must be five hundred thousand people in Puerto Rico named Perez."

"That's all I know."

"If this Perez was in San Juan, why did Ike go to the Garden last night?"

"I didn't know he went there until the police told me," Pinchos said. "I thought he had already left for San Juan."

"You must have read the papers today about Carmelo Fischetti. Did you know him?"

"No."

"What about a girl named Ileana?"

He swallowed and took a drag on the cigarette. The strong odor of its smoke permeated the room.

"I met her once or twice," he said, in a cautious way. "Just hello and how are you."

"Was Ike having an affair with her?"

"Possibly. But I don't know for certain. I'm the
. . ."

"The inside man. Sure . . ."

I picked up some of the tools that had fallen
to the floor, and then stared past the bars, into the
airshaft. The gun felt heavy in my pocket. Then
I picked up the photograph of Ike with the rabbi.
The glass was cracked across Ike's face.

"Who's this?" I said.

"It's Rabbi Kotz," he said, as if the name alone
explained everything.

"Who is Rabbi Kotz?"

"You are fooling with me, no?"

"No, I don't know Rabbi Kotz from a bottle of
Manischewitz."

He winced at the irreverence.

"The *rebbe* is the head of the Marovicher
Hasidim in Brooklyn. He is one of the most important Jewish leaders in the world."

I looked at the photograph again. The face was
vaguely familiar, and old images of the same man
floated around in my head like leaflets from a
forgotten political campaign: posing with mayors
and senators and an endless parade of candidates
wearing yarmulkes, making demands and extract-
ing promises from all of them. The demands were
always simple: nuke Hanoi, get more cops on the
streets, and stop abortion. He and two or three
other Hasidic rabbis were courted every election
year, because their people lived together, prayed
together, and most of all, voted together.

"I've never met the man," I said carefully. "Tell
me about him."

"He traces his ancestry to the beginnings of the

Hasidic movement in the seventeenth century," he said gravely. "He is considered a *tzaddik*, a holy man, by all who know him. He is descended in a direct line from the first *tzaddik* of Marovich."

"Where's he from?"

"He arrived here from Hungary in 1946, a survivor of the camps. The Holocaust had taught him even more to passionately love God. He opened his first yeshiva in Williamsburg, in Brooklyn, in the cellar of a tenement. He had exactly four pupils. Today there are more than five thousand pupils in our community, in many different yeshivas. We have our own pharmacy. Our own bakery. Our own police and ambulance patrols." His voice expanded with pride. "We even have our own bus service too, which brings the men each day from Brooklyn to Forty-seventh Street and then takes them home in the evening. And, oh, yes, we run a medical clinic and a dental clinic."

"So you're a Marovicher too?"

"Not a very good one," he said. "But I try."

"What would the *tzaddik* say if he knew that you had a part in stealing one of the most important pieces of jewelry in Jewish history?"

"It's not stolen!"

"Then where the hell is it, pal?"

He turned his eyes away, reached over to the jeweler's table and picked a Kleenex out of a box. He blew his nose, with studied deliberation. "I don't believe Ike would steal from me. He was still enough of a Jew not to steal."

"You're starting to whine, Pinchos," I said. "You're a better man than that."

"Perhaps I was once," he said. "Long ago. When I was young and thin and wanted to live."

I waited for him to say something else. Instead he just sat there, as if locked in a cell. I asked quietly, "Tell me where you got the piece."

He took off his glasses and rubbed them with a dry corner of the Kleenex.

"It's a long story," he said.

10.

The story started at the end of the Yom Kippur War. Lev Pinchos had been called up with the other reserves, too old now to fight very much, but experienced enough to work as a field nurse. And he found himself tending a young soldier named Arieh in a field hospital in the Sinai. Arieh had been in a tank that was hit by a rocket, and for one long afternoon the doctors had worked steadily to piece him together. When they had done all they could do, Pinchos stayed with the young man, speaking to him late into the night, as the Israelis leaped the Canal and drove into Egypt. Arieh was nineteen, and in too much pain to sleep. Then, loaded with morphine, the boy started to tell Lev Pinchos about what had happened to him and his girl friend two years earlier on a weekend archaeological dig near the town of Nablis on the West Bank.

"The night before the dig, they had stayed up very late," Pinchos said. "Making plans for their lives. They knew it would not be an easy life. The boy was a Yemeni, a black Israeli, and very poor.

Rebecca was a sabra, born in Israel of survivors of the Holocaust. Her parents both worked in some minor government ministry. But for those young people, life was not going to be easy, and they knew it. They were drawn to archaeology, he told me, because they were convinced that he was a Canaanite, a direct descendant of those who lived in Israel before even the arrival of the Hebrews. Somehow he thought that archaeology would make him the equal of any other Israeli. He was convinced of that, and so was she."

He lit another brown-papered cigarette, his face cloudy and troubled. Something about the story began to feel false; it was being laid out too neatly, and it was getting slippery with sentiment. But I didn't interrupt.

"In the morning, the last day of their weekend, they began again to dig. It was still dark and cool. And they began to find things. First some earthen cups, lined with some metal. Probably ancient *kiddush* cups, for wine. They kept digging. And then they found a small metal box. It must have been copper that had oxidized, because Arieh said it was encrusted with a substance as rough and hard as stone, and they could not open it, even after hitting it with shovels and with rocks. They dug all the rest of the morning, but found only broken shards and some pieces of crumbling brick. They took what they had found and went home."

"Isn't that against Israeli law?" I said. "Taking things home from a dig?"

"Of course," Pinchos said, "and the boy and girl knew it. But he was obsessed with this thing about legitimacy. He thought that something inside that box might be the proof. On the following day, he brought home tools from the carpenter's shop where he worked, and he opened the box. And the piece was there."

"Did he know what it was?"

"No. But the girl knew it was very special. She talked about it as if it were a gift from God. It would be their inheritance, something that would establish them in the world when it was time to marry. She would never have to get help from relatives. They had a gift. At that time, she was in school. They would wait until she graduated. Then they would leave Israel, take this great gift to America, sell it to someone rich, and have enough money to get them started in life."

He laughed in a dry, bitter way.

"Things began to go wrong soon after that," he said. "The girl's father died in a car crash. Her mother had a second heart attack, lingered awhile, and then she was gone too. The girl was left alone in the apartment in Tel Aviv. The boy blamed the breastplate for the turn of events. She said no, it could not be that, that this was the modern world, all the rest is superstition. And besides, she said, it must be worth at least twenty thousand dollars."

"How much *is* it worth?"

"Name a number from fifty million and up," he said sadly. "The problem is locating the perfect buyer. It must be someone who wants it only for himself. Someone who would never display it. Never tell friends about it. Someone who realized that as soon as he revealed it to the world, he would have to reveal where it came from, and then he would have to return it to its owners."

"The people of Israel."

"The government of Israel," he said acidly.

"And how did you get it?" I said. I could feel the other half of me, the Catholic half, rising up and taking over; I was becoming your friendly neighborhood priest, receiving a general confession so that the penitent could make his Easter duty. Barry Fitzgerald with a yarmulke.

"He told me where it was, that dying boy," Pinchos said, his voice coming from a long distance away. "He told me of the flat in Tel Aviv. Where the girl lived. Rebecca. And that afternoon, the boy died. The next day, the war was over. And three days later, I was sent home. My mind was inflamed with possibility. I didn't care if what I contemplated was against the laws of Israel. I had fought three times for Israel. In 1948, in 1956, in 1967. I had done what I must do, I had been shot . . ."

He lifted his pants leg, and showed a sickly white scar running from his knee to the top of his white socks.

". . . I had suffered. And after many years of honest work, I was earning less than two hundred dollars a week, as a master craftsman. I had done my duty. And now something enormous had been described to me by a dying boy in the sands of the Sinai. I was a jeweler. I knew the history of my profession. And I was certain that he had found the breastplate of Aaron. I was overwhelmed."

He jammed the cigarette butt against the sole of his shoe, and then shoved his hands almost forlornly into the pockets of his trousers.

"For two days, I watched the house," he said. "Sitting in a corner café, reading the newspapers. I saw the girl leave at precisely the same time

89

every morning, presumably to go to work. On the third day, I brought some tools, and broke in rather easily. I went through the place very methodically, and in the bedroom, under the bed, there were some loose boards. I lifted them. A parcel wrapped in cheap brown paper was lying there. I tore the strings and the paper off, and there it was. After thirty-three centuries."

"How did you know it was real?"

"When I held it in my hand," he said. "It was as if I had communicated directly with Yahweh himself."

The elevator suddenly cranked and heaved in its shaft. We both leaned at the same angle, trying to see around the corner of the L-shaped room. I could see a sliver of light as the elevator passed 11, heading to the street floor.

"You expecting anyone?"

His face was puffy with alarm.

"No."

"Stay right where you are," I said. I got up and put out all the lights, holding the gun in my hand. Then I got down behind the jeweler's bench, with a clear shot at the elevator. I could see Pinchos off to my left, clearly silhouetted against the window.

The elevator started again. It was coming up.

I heard Pinchos breathing hard.

If they were coming to this floor, they would need keys to get through the gate. But there was an easier way: they could shoot that lock off. If they had an automatic, they would have no problem. If they had gas . . . Pinchos held his breath. The elevator went past our floor, going to some place above us. I heard it stop, its doors open and close again. Pinchos breathed out hard and then breathed in, and then wheezed. I switched on a small cowled lamp over the designer's bench.

"You should get a shade for that window," I said.

"I should get many things."

"Finish the story," I said.

"There isn't much to tell," he said. His voice was now drained and remote. "I took the piece and went home. And then I went about my work as if nothing had happened. I looked at the newspapers every day for a week but there wasn't a word in them about the robbery. Obviously the girl could not report the theft to the police because she was not supposed to have the piece in the first place. And I didn't think I had sinned. I had robbed a robber, *nu*? For three months, I saved money. And then I came to New York."

"How did you get it through customs?"

He rubbed his thumb and his forefinger together. "There are ways."

"There usually are."

"All through those first few years, I waited," he said, proud of his own patience. "I was learning how the business worked. And I knew I needed a partner, preferably an American. One day, I was hunched over a cheap diamond, examining its flaws —it was dreck from the Urals—when I looked up from the loupe and saw Ike. He had been told to look me up for some small job. Ten minutes later, I knew I had found my partner."

"Why?"

"He was a tough Jew."

"That he was. The best Brownsville knows how to make. Or did."

"And now . . ."

He shrugged, looking melancholy and wasted. I asked him to open the gate.

"What are you going to do?" he said.

"Find Ike," I said, and buzzed the elevator. The car was empty, so I handed the gun back to Pinchos and went down to the street.

11.

A uniformed cop stood in the side door of Brentano's, copping a furtive smoke, but the rest of Forty-seventh Street was empty. I walked west, past all the shuttered jewelry stores with their hidden treasures of glittering dreams. Now I knew that there was what Hitchcock once called a Maguffin: a thing, an object, a prize for which people might kill each other. It had come across the centuries, and now it was touching strangers; it had even touched me. It was part of a sickness to which I'd thought I was immune.

The jewelry thing had never meant anything to me. When I walked Fifth Avenue with my first and only wife, she would drift to the gold and diamonds in the windows of Tiffany's or Forty-seventh Street, and I would drift to the bookstores. She would talk about the brilliance of these tiny pieces of cut stone, their durability, their luster, their fire. She would tell me in a marveling voice how amber and jet came from plants, while pearl and coral came from the sea, and all the rest came from the fluted airholes of dead volcanoes, under the crust of the earth. She talked with awe about diamonds; I wanted to discuss Simenon or Stendhal. Perhaps she could have hooked me with the wars that had been fought for such treasure; the fortunes that were built on those stones drawn from the earth by black men; by the crimes committed for their possession. But she didn't, and I never cared. And now I was involved; touched by a thing from the ancient past, made in the headwaters of the Jewish stream, part of my own past, in some awful cosmic way; a thing that had probably just killed two people on a single night, and might kill more. And now I had picked up the disease, because now I wanted to see it for myself, to hold it in my hands, to study it and weigh it. I had traveled a long way from those days when the woman I loved drifted to the jewelry shops and I drifted to the bookshops before we drifted apart for good.

I went into the parking garage, paid for the car, and called Marta from the phone in the waiting room. She answered on the first ring.

"You okay?" she said.

"Yeah. Anything I should know?"

"One big thing, and a lot of little things. The big thing is that Ileana Martinez lists her address at 23 Bay Sixteenth Street in Coney Island. That's down the block from the headquarters of Monon Perez and his little empire."

I let the words hang there in the closed air of the phone booth.

That was the connection. It was too close to be an accident and too loose for an indictment. But it was something.

"Meet me downstairs in ten minutes," I said.

"Should I bring a bathing suit?"

"It's not warm enough."

"It never is," she said and hung up.

I drove up Eleventh Avenue until it became West End. There was nothing new on the news. Some stations had already dropped the story. The cops were obviously playing their cards close to the vest. Carmelo Fischetti, Ileana Martinez, Ike Roth, Monon Perez: all came to the Garden. Carmelo got himself dead. Ike vanished, and was supposed to see a man named Perez in San Juan. Sarah was killed and I was skulled. And Ileana was somehow connected to Monon Perez. It all fit together somehow, but I wasn't sure how.

Marta was standing under the awning when I reached Eighty-fifth Street. She was wearing a red turtleneck sweater, a denim jacket and blue jeans and her teeth were very white when she smiled. She opened the door and got in, squashing her long body deep into the seat, and putting one white-sandaled foot on the dashboard. Her toenails were painted coral.

"Where to, señor?" she said.

"The beach, of course."

I drove down the West Side and told her most of what I knew. I left out the breastplate; if she didn't know about it, maybe nobody would try to hurt her to get it. She listened in silence, as we passed under the rusting hulk of the old highway, and rushed past the rotting piers. The gay boys were out in force outside the Anvil and the Meat Rack, pursuing leather dreams, and there were a few lone hookers in ten-year-old miniskirts waiting for truckdrivers near the Holland Tunnel. I was wondering about Ike and Ileana, and what they did in the night, and then scrubbed the images away as we moved into the Brooklyn Battery Tunnel. I felt flat and empty and didn't talk. The traffic was suddenly dense again, and Marta rolled up the windows. This was what purgatory must be like: trapped beneath the sea in an endless tunnel, with gasoline engines pumping poison into the air, while tunnel cops with glass chests opened their shirts at forty-five-foot intervals, to show off their brown lungs. Marta lit a cigarette, as we came up out of the tunnel at last, paid the toll, and swung onto the Belt Parkway.

"You're looking for Monon, right?" she said.

"Right."

"Suppose you find him?"

"I hope I do. One thing is certain: he won't take my calls. I have to go there in the flesh."

"But what do you think he'll say? That he's a killer?"

"No. But he'll say something. He's the kind has to talk about what he does. Women, larceny, murder. If he doesn't talk about it, he didn't do it. It's part of the style."

"Turtle doesn't talk, does he?"

"Turtle never talks."

We could see the great double arc of the Verrazano Bridge now, stretching from Bay Ridge across the Narrows to Staten Island, where lines of blinking lights marched over the rolling hills and ridges. A black freighter churned slowly to anchor, guided by two squat tugs.

"Are you okay, Sam?" Marta said softly.

"Yeah."

"You don't sound okay."

I glanced at her, and saw her face staring at me. I said: "I'm sorry. I'm trying to fit all of this

96

together. I'm an unpleasant bastard when I'm thinking."

"I've seen you when you're thinking. You're not thinking now. Not at all."

"You're right. I'm not thinking."

"Then I'll talk, okay?"

"Okay."

She told me about Ileana, and how Ileana had met Monon Perez one night at the Corso; how she had come on strong to Monon, and got caught up with him, and wasn't seen around the Corso without him. She told me about Monon's wife, a woman named Carmen ("They're always called Carmen"), who had come up with Monon from Puerto Rico years before, had helped him along, worked for him, and then gotten older and heavier while Monon drank more frequently from the fountain of young ladies.

"Carmen waited just past that age when she might have left him and started over," Marta said. "So when he began making the big money, they came to an agreement. She didn't care who he played around with as long as she didn't get embarrassed, and as long as he took care of her with money."

She took some papers out of her handbag.

"So Monon took care of her," she said. "There's a finca outside Ponce, down in P.R. It's in her name. There are some cars there, and a boat, all in her name. A company in her name owns a helicopter that flies charter flights around the island. She has cattle in her name in Jersey and some land in the Dominican Republic. It's all part of the big pie. And it's good for Monon. If the Feds come around, or the cops, or the son-of-a-bitch reporters, everything's in the name of good old Carmen."

"The money really was huge, wasn't it?" I said. My voice sounded flat and distant. I didn't like the way it sounded.

"He's got this umbrella organization, the one in Coney Island, the Greater Brooklyn Development Corporation," she said. "That controls more than thirty smaller outfits. He has to cut in various people, but that's just overhead. When he has paid off everybody, Monon personally controls about twelve million dollars a year."

"That's a lot of arroz con pollo," I said.

"Feel any better?"

"No."

"The pieces are falling together, though, aren't they?" she said. "Ileana and Monon. It makes you think. Your cousin Ike thought he was boffing Ileana, but probably Monon was boffing Ike. Real good."

I laughed. "And the boffing you get is not worth the boffing you get."

"Now you look better. You always look better when you laugh."

"It's just a nervous tic from the pain in my skull."

"You wanna park and neck?"

"Sure."

"But the hat's gotta go. Where'd you get that thing? Off a corpse?"

"I wore it the first Christmas I was home from the Navy, so nobody'd laugh at my skinned head."

"Pull over, Briscoe. I want your body."

"After we see Monon."

Then the bridge was behind us, and the highway

moved in a long curve to the east, and up ahead I could see the lights of the ferris wheel in Coney Island.

"Open the glove compartment," I said.

She snapped it open.

"Under those maps is a .45 caliber Colt Automatic," I said. "It is loaded. I have a license to carry it. Put it in your purse."

"You've got to be kidding."

She rummaged around and found the gun. I kept my eyes on the road, watching for the Stillwell Avenue exit.

"You won't have to use it. Probably."

"I never used one of these things in my life," she said.

"There's a doodad there called a safety," I said. "If you have to use it, move the safety to the side. Then there's a thing called a trigger. You just point it at someone and squeeze the trigger. It's easy. Every teenager in New York has one."

"What the hell are you getting me into, Briscoe?"

"Hey," I said, "these are your people, not mine."

"Then you shoot them, schmuck. I don't want to look bad in *El Diario*."

"If we're lucky, nobody will shoot anybody. Put it in the handbag."

I got off at Stillwell Avenue and pulled around into Coney Island. I wished I could explain to Marta that this had once been Disneyland and Vegas and the Riviera, all in one place, when I was a kid: a gorgeous, noisy, vulgar paradise that smelled of salt and hot corn and frying hotdogs and knishes. I would try to make her see my father standing at the bar at Scoville's with the other cops, their sports shirts covering the guns, and the women out back sitting at the tables under the umbrellas. The cops would slip me quarters and I'd go running with the other kids the five blocks to Nathan's, where the hotdogs were still a nickel and the watermelon sign promised that a slice would wash your face, brush your teeth and clean your ears. She would see all of that: and the men drinking beer from giant iced pitchers, and eating mounds of fried clams, and sometimes fighting each other in the sandy alley behind the restaurant. The women sat at the tables, or went to the beach with the kids, and unfurled great blankets and spread giant feasts of chicken and cold cuts, potato salad and soda. If I had words for it, I would tell Marta about the way my mother looked in those summers, her skin pink from the sun, wearing a straw hat with a yellow ribbon that floated in the breeze, and the way my father held the chair for her when she sat down and how happy and pleased she was when he would join the other cops and sing Irish songs with the phrasing of a Brownsville Jew. Driving slowly now on Surf Avenue, I remembered all that: and a summer years later when I was in love with a girl from Oceantide, up the boardwalk from Scoville's, a thin pretty girl who didn't love me back, but who danced with me while Joni James sang "Have You Heard?" from the jukebox. That was the summer Ike Roth came home from the Army and took me to Ebbetts Field for a night game and bought me three illegal beers and told me how he was going to be a rich man someday, in the diamond business. I laughed and said I didn't want to be rich, I just wanted to draw cartoons for the

The Deadly Piece

Journal-American or write sports for the *Brooklyn Eagle*. And now the *Eagle* and the *Journal-American* were dead, and the Dodgers were gone, and Ebbetts Field was a housing project with a sign that said NO BALL PLAYING ALLOWED. One year, they came around with bulldozers and shoveled Scoville's off the earth, and another year my father was killed, going after a holdup man in a joint in Brownsville, and my mother had finished her last painful years in a hospital and the places where they all had lived in Brownsville had fallen into rubble from too much arson and too much indifference. Oceantide was a ruin. The thin pretty girl had married someone else. And Coney Island wasn't a paradise anymore for anyone. It was dope and welfare and bitterness, ruled over by people like Monon Perez.

"It's all changed," I said, looking out at the rubble-strewn streets.

"Everything does," she said.

"Yeah," I said. "But not for the best."

12.

The Greater Brooklyn Development Corporation was housed in a squat, gloomy pile that filled most of the city block across the street from the Half Moon Hotel. In the murky darkness, it looked like a farewell job from the architect of the Bastille. Three stories rose from the littered sidewalk, with the windows on the left climbing two stories, and all the windows covered with grilles. Fire stairs ran down one side, but clearly you would have as much trouble breaking out as you would have breaking in. An old-fashioned water tank sat on the roof like a fat, brutal sentry. The walls were made of granite, turned a mucous gray by years of sea air. There were a few lights burning in the upper story. A huge sign had been stretched over the double doors of the main entrance, announcing in capital letters that this was the Greater Brooklyn Development Corporation, Monon H. Perez, President. The slogan "Progress Through Cooperation" had been added, bracketed in quote marks that seemed sarcastic comments by the sign painter.

"It's a beautiful piece of work," Marta said, as I turned the corner. "Early Sing-Sing Modern."

I came to Neptune Avenue and remembered suddenly what the building had been in the old days.

"That's the baths!" I said. "The Old Neptune Baths. Well, I'll be damned. When I was a kid, it was a big, fancy place, with lines outside on the weekends, locker rooms, steam baths, the whole act."

I saw empty yards behind the building, and then some decaying two-family houses. An abandoned tenement stood mutely across the street, its blind eyes staring at the desolation. There were a few parked cars, and a few that had been left to die on the streets, the tires gone, the windshields punched in, the chrome scarred and rusted. I circled the block and came back to Surf Avenue. There were lights burning in the Half Moon Hotel. Old people lived there now, but years ago, Abe Reles had been thrown to his death from an upper story a few days before he was to testify about the bravos of Murder Incorporated. I could never pass that building without thinking of the racket guys from Georgia and Livonia, who had shot their way out of poverty right into the electric chair. I parked the car under a streetlight in front of the hotel, in the block between Surf Avenue and the boardwalk. A special guard dozed in the lobby. I locked the car and gave the keys to Marta. I could hear the long roar of the sea.

"Let's see if anyone's home up the block," I said.

The double doors of the Greater Brooklyn Development Corporation were sheathed in hammered tin, streaked with rust where the nails had been driven. I pounded on the door, like a cop making a raid, and Marta smiled and hugged her handbag. Nobody answered. I pounded the door again, and then kicked it, and finally heard bolts being shoved aside angrily. The door opened. The little asp from Madison Square Garden stood there. He didn't seem to recognize me. Behind him was a large lobby-sized room, with posters on all the walls, advertising educational programs and welfare-rights meetings. A large portrait of Monon was hung over the arch of a stairway leading to the upper floors.

"What the hell are you, crazy?" the asp said.

"Where's Monon, pally?"

"He ain't here, and—"

Suddenly, he recognized me, and a hand went involuntarily to his throat and he started to close the door. I shoved him backwards and walked in. His hand went for a pocket and I kicked him hard in the knee, grabbed his shirt with both hands, whipped him around, and slammed him into the stone wall. He froze in shock. I reached into his pocket and found the shiv. It was an ivory-handled switchblade about eight inches long. I pressed the button and the blade whipped out. The asp's eyes widened, but he made no sound. I folded the knife. His jaw was hanging open now, and I shoved the folded switchblade into his mouth.

"Now call Monon," I said.

He tried to say something, and then Marta started to laugh. I turned, and she was bending over, laughing hysterically and banging the sandstone walls with an open hand.

"You're nuts, Briscoe. You're a maniac!"

"I just wanted to say hello," I said, and slid the

knife out of his mouth, and dropped in into my pocket. The asp stood there. There was no fight in him at all. The asp had become just another scared kid.

"All right, *chamaco*, where's your boss?" I said.

The kid's eyes shot to the stairs, but he didn't say anything. Marta had stopped laughing.

"Marta, you got the gun?" I said, turning to her, and winking. She slid the .45 out of her handbag, hefting it as if she'd been using it for ten years. Panic darted through the kid's eyes.

"Hey, I got nothin' to do with this," he said in a choked, small voice. "I jus' work here, man."

"Shut up," I said, and opened one of the double doors. I could see Red Emma parked under the streetlight in front of the Half Moon Hotel, but no traffic moved along Surf Avenue.

"Now stand over there," I said to the kid. He stood with his back against the unopened side of the double doors. Marta looked at him, an amused twinkle in her eyes.

I told her: "Stand in that open door, so you can watch the street. If I'm not downstairs in fifteen minutes, shoot this bum."

"It'll be a pleasure," she said, her face grim and her eyes smiling. She pulled the bag to her side so that it hid the gun from anyone passing in the street.

"Try to kill him with one shot," I said. "Make it painless."

"Aw, I'd rather shoot him a little at a time."

"Suit yourself."

I went up the flight of sandstone steps. There was a moldy smell of dampness oozing from the old stones. The bare walls were painted the pale green you see in police stations and municipal hospitals, but they bubbled with flaky mold in places, and felt scabby to the touch. I reached the second floor and found myself in a long corridor. A slice of light showed under a door at the far end. Another short stairway moved to the top floor, and I could hear the heavy click of pool balls and murmurous conversation in Spanish. I walked down the dark corridor to where the light showed, and knocked on the door.

There was a beat of silence. Then: *"Quien é?"*

"Sam Briscoe."

"Who?" the voice said again in Spanish.

"Un reportero."

I heard feet shuffling to the door. I braced myself, expecting a rush. If my luck was really running bad, Turtle would be in there, ready to eat me for dinner. I heard the lock tumble and then the door opened swiftly. A pale, sallow man looked at me, his eyes blinking, adjusting to the darkness. He was wearing a green wool cap, and white starched shirt, gray slacks and polished brown shoes. He was in his fifties.

"Who are you?" I said.

"Escudo," he said. "Who are you?"

"Briscoe," I said, without elaborating. "Where's Monon?"

"Mr. Perez is not here."

I moved past him and closed the door and locked it. He backed up. We filled the empty spaces of the small room. There was a tiny couch, its leatherette covering flaked with wear. A row of file cabinets were against one wall, a small table was wedged against a second door, and a large, battered desk filled the rest of the cramped space. A cowled lamp was set over the desk, and there were accountant's ledgers spread out where Escudo obviously had been working. A box of toothpicks was set beside a bottle of Waterman's blue-black ink. A small pile of broken toothpicks half-filled an ashtray.

"Trying to give up smoking?" I said, rolling a toothpick between thumb and forefinger.

"Yes," he said in Spanish. "It's a very hard thing to do, when you're at work."

"You're the accountant?"

"I am an accountant."

"Very interesting," I said. "You must know where the money went."

He shrugged his shoulders, snapped a toothpick, moved around the desk to his chair. I moved before him, and opened the drawer. No gun. Just paperclips, rubber bands, erasing fluid, and some pencils. An accountant's armory.

"Monon isn't here?" I said.

"He went to Puerto Rico," he said in Spanish. His accent betrayed him.

"You're Dominican?" I said.

He shrugged and snapped a toothpick.

"I see, said the blind man." He wouldn't look at me. "You're *indocumentado*, right? An illegal. Arrived here without papers. And you work for Monon, because he knows you can't go to the cops, because they'll lock you up for being here illegally. So you keep the books the way Monon tells you to keep them. Do I have it right?"

He sighed, and diddled with a pen. I looked at the files.

"Are they locked?"

"No."

"I'll help myself," I said. I opened the drawers and most of them were filled with junk. Letters from prisoners asking for help. Letters from residents of Brooklyn who wanted fire hydrants turned on or shut off; potholes filled; summer jobs for their kids; nursing homes for their parents. It was the usual accumulation of large and small griefs. In my years at a newspaper, I'd seen all the same letters.

A few drawers were empty. And one drawer was locked. I turned to Escudo.

"*La llave, amigo,*" I said. "The key."

He paused, looked at the door, as if expecting the arrival of the cavalry. But there was no sound. The room was hotter now, and I was aware of some large, bulging wet force in the building. He opened a side drawer and took out a key, labeled with a disc of orange paper. He tossed it to me, and sat down.

I opened the drawer. It held a single file folder, an inch thick, marked "Jews." I laid it on the table that was shoved in front of the second door, and started to go through it. It was a dossier of various Jewish leaders: rabbis, politicians, businessmen. Each was typed on green paper, and listed the addresses, home and business telephone numbers, known real-estate properties, estimated value of those properties, political affiliations, and the amount of poverty funds, if any, going to the subject's organizations.

In addition, there were tearsheets from the *Jewish Press*, the conservative weekly, showing Monon posing with various rabbis and other leaders, and ads paid for by Monon on Jewish religious holidays. One even congratulated the Israeli government on the raid at Entebbe. There were also a handful of letters and notes. Most of them were simple expressions of thanks, some addressed to Monon and his wife, for showing up at bar mitzvahs or fundraisers. But one of them was different. It was a piece of stationery with Hebrew lettering at the top, identifying the Archaeological Bureau of the State of Israel. The message was written in a rolling feminine handwriting. It said:

> M. Perez,
> *I am thrilled at the latest news. I am making arrangements to come to America at the soonest possible date, and will contact you upon arrival. I will bring the agreed amount of cash for your brother.*

It was not signed.

I folded the note and slipped it into my hip pocket. I went back to the other files, looking under the K's for Kotz comma Mendel comma Rabbi.

And then someone knocked on the door.

13.

"Escudo! Open this goddamned door!"

I knew the voice, and so did Escudo. It was the voice of the Turtle, and it was loud in the land. Escudo's eyes were on the door, but he didn't move. I had a sudden vision of Marta's face, broken and hurt. I looked at the second door, with the table in front of it.

"What's out there?" I whispered.

Escudo just blinked.

Turtle's voice was louder now: "Who the hell is in there wit' you, Escudo?"

The handle of the door jiggled violently.

"Get up!" I said hoarsely. Escudo stood up, with fear in his eyes, as Turtle shouted: "I'm coming through this thing, Escudo!"

Escudo looked at me, as if for help, and I hit him as hard as I could on the chin. He went over the arm of the couch, without making a sound, his feet pointing at the ceiling. Unconscious, he might be safe from Turtle.

I pulled the table away from the second door. There was a simple bolt holding it shut, but it was rusted and corroded. I tried to move it with my hand, and it didn't budge. I heard Turtle slam into the other door. I stepped back and kicked at the lock, and it came right off. I shoved the door, which opened out, ready to run down a corridor.

And found myself fifty feet above a giant swimming pool. The strong smell of chlorine stung my eyes, and eerie shadows moved along the tile walls from the huge green rectangle below. I was unbalanced, teetered, started to fall, then grabbed the door frame. Down below, a great wide terrace was built around the edges of the pool. It must have held hundreds of bathers through those winters when the Neptune Baths were in their glory. But if I had kept going out the door, I'd have landed on that terrace, not in the pool, and they'd have buried me with an eyedropper.

A rusting iron catwalk ran from this door around the room. On the far side, opposite me, was another door. They must have used the catwalk in the old days to scrub the upper walls and the ceilings. It was about a foot wide, made of thin iron slats bolted to the walls. I heard Turtle hit the office door again, and I stepped down onto the catwalk.

There were no handholds, and the walls were wet with condensation. I went along one wall, with the catwalk trembling beneath me. I turned the corner. And then it suddenly fell away beneath me. I reached out, grabbed for a piece of rusting iron, heard a loud caroming clatter as a piece of the catwalk hit the terrace fifty feet below. And I hung there.

I started to pull myself up, afraid to swing, afraid to add more weight to the piece of catwalk.

The rusted iron dug into the palms of my hands. And then I heard a violent slamming, tearing sound from inside the office, and I knew that Turtle had broken through. I heaved, struggled, and pulled myself up, chest high with the catwalk. I reached forward, grabbed another rung, and hooked a knee onto the walkway. I could see the great rough dimples where the bolts had pulled out of the walls. It was very quiet, except for the lapping of the green water, far below.

"Briscoe!"

Turtle's voice echoed in the green shimmering room. I was on my knees on the catwalk and saw his bullet-like head peering around the door frame.

"Is that a cigar in your mouth, Turtle, or are you taking a shit?"

He smiled at me. "You better come back here, Briscoe."

"Why don't you come and get me, fat man?"

He looked down at the broken hunk of catwalk, and then at me: "Maybe I'll just shoot you and make it easy."

"That'll be swell, Turtle. But there's some cops waiting for me around the corner who would love to boil your corn. Shoot me, and they'll be here before the bullets hit."

"Just come back the way you came," he said.

"Nah, I don't think so. I think I'll just keep going the way I was going. It's a great view. I'm the only man in America who ever saw Monon Perez' private swimming pool." I started moving along the ledge, and kept talking; if I kept talking maybe he wouldn't remember to shoot me. All I wanted to do was reach that other door. "You have lifeguards here, Turtle? Who pays, the Feds, state or city?"

"I think you're fulla shit about the cops. I don't think there's no cops out there."

"That's a double negative, Turtle. It means there really are cops outside."

"I don't believe you."

"Why don't you go look?" I said. "And while you're at it, why don't you go down to Philadelphia and get me some cream cheese."

I turned the corner, walking carefully, my back to the wall.

"You talk a lot, don't you?" he said.

The gun was hanging at his side now.

"If I have to, I do more than talk, Turtle. I could, for example, knock you on your ass."

"You and what army?"

"Army?" I said, and faked a laugh. "Hell, Turtle, you're too old now. You're fat and slow. You're not in shape anymore, fat man. You've lost that competitive edge. It comes from beating up women and children."

"I'd eat you for breakfast, punk."

"You don't have the heart, Turtle," I said.

I was twenty feet from the other door now. If it was locked, I was dead. "That's why you have to carry a piece. You can't do it with your hands anymore. You're a punk now, Turtle. A no-heart punk."

Suddenly, he was gone. I heard the office door slam. He was coming around to meet me at this final door. I hurried, felt the catwalk begin to give again and froze, my hands on the scummy wall. This had to be an exit. It had to lead to a hall, or a fire stairs. It just had to. And Turtle would have to go downstairs, maybe, and come back upstairs, maybe, and find a key, maybe, if it was locked, or go all the way to the roof and come down again if it led that way. Maybe. I moved one long step, tested the strength of the catwalk. It seemed to hold. Then another long step. And then a third. I grabbed for the door handle.

And the door swung open.

I was suspended for a second. Nothing to hold. Nothing to keep myself from falling. Nothing to keep me alive. I was going to die. Right now.

And then Turtle reached out and grabbed me by the shirt front and pulled me to him and clubbed me with a fist. It was like being hit with a leather bag of BB's.

"I'll give you 'punk'," he said, and clubbed me again, holding me with that one powerful hand, my legs dangling free. My hat flew off with the first punch and then my head exploded from another clubbing punch and then another and then another. He was going to beat me to death in mid-air and then let me fall. He was the strongest human being I'd ever met.

"Punk," he grunted. "Punk."

I grabbed his outstretched arm, the one that was holding me in the air. It was like grabbing a branch of an oak tree. I saw his eyes, fevered and full of mad pleasure, and then I remembered his best move, and was afraid he would now clamp those teeth around my ears, and spit them one at a time into the swimming pool.

I held his arm, swung my legs in until they touched the ledge, and then pushed.

We went off together, Turtle on top of me, the

two of us tumbling through the air, my brain dazed and hurting.

There was a sudden startling swashing sound and then we were in the water and I was moving freely. The shock of the water cleared my head. I touched bottom and shoved myself back to the surface.

I couldn't see Turtle.

I paddled toward the edge of the pool, my shoes heavy with water, my breath coming in long strangled draughts. I reached the glistening ceramic edge of the pool. And then my ankles were caught in an iron grip and I was sucked under.

I kicked my feet downwards but Turtle's hands were locked on my ankles and he was dragging me through the green water to the deepest end of the pool. I doubled under at the waist, trying to grab at him, touched his head, couldn't get a grip, and then he let go, and I shot to the surface, gasping for air. I saw Turtle's face, fifteen feet away, about to go under again. He ripped off his shirt. His eyes were hunter's eyes now, cold and immune. And then he was gone, the shirt floating on the surface, and I sensed him coming for me and kicked. He caught my right foot. My shoe came off in his hand, but then he had the other ankle and he was drawing me down again, into the dark, tepid greenness.

I twisted and bent and dove at him, seeing only a blurry pink shape. I slammed my head at the shape, but hit nothing. Our motions grew slower now in the soundless water. I tried to butt him again, hit something, then saw him more clearly, thumped him again with my head, and he let go, and moved away, looking rubbery and strong, like some new species of mammal. I tried to swim up to the light, hoping I had stunned him, and had almost reached the surface when the hand clamped me again and started me down into the darkness. My lungs were starting to spasm, wanting to draw in air, kept shut only because my brain had locked them shut. I tried to go up, and he pulled me deeper. I felt my throat try to open, told it to stay shut, felt it open again, told it again. And then I was very tired, my bones dissolving, floating into a pale green dream, going deeper and deeper, feeling lazy and drowsy, a singing sound in my ears.

And I remembered the knife.

The asp's knife.

The knife in my pocket.

I saw Turtle now, his great hulk settled on the bottom. He was holding one of my ankles in each hand. His mouth was clamped shut. Tiny bubbles rose in a wavering line from his nose. I jerked one of my legs, and he reached up and gripped my knee. He started climbing my body. He was about to make his move. I went limp and let him come.

A hand grasped my thigh. And then he vaulted ahead, propelling himself toward my face, as I opened the knife in my pocket. He reached for my throat. And I slashed at him with the open blade.

Suddenly the water was the color of diluted wine. There was a great churning and thrashing and I couldn't see him anymore. I rose, burst through the surface, and gulped for the sweet, beautiful air.

He broke the surface fifteen feet away. A terrible, howling, wounded sound came from him, like a

116

seal being slaughtered, and I could see the slice across his naked chest and up the shoulder and the layer of white fat and the welling blood. He howled, and went under, and came up again, and howled.

I dragged myself over the edge of the pool, gasping and choking, fighting down the vomit. Turtle went under again. The door upstairs flopped on its hinge and I looked up and saw Escudo standing there, very still, a spectator of things in a country that was not his own.

There were six doors along the pool edge, and I started to try them. Turtle came up again, not seeing me, floundering in his pain, trying to get to the edge of the pool. The third door opened into a long, dark corridor with dim squares of light at the end. I moved into the darkness. My shoe made a squishing sound and I kicked it off. The squares were set into one of those fire doors with a long horizontal bar that you push down to get out. I pushed it down and staggered into the night.

I found myself in a small yard at the rear of the building. The rusting frame of a child's swing stood against a fence. I lifted myself up on the crossbar, leaned out and grabbed the top of the wooden fence. I stood for a moment and then dropped into the street on the other side.

Surf Avenue was to my left. The Half Moon Hotel was on the next block, across the avenue. I crossed the street to the abandoned tenement, dodging broken glass and asphalt. I huddled in a doorway, my eyes adjusting to the darkness. Then I saw four young men come around the corner in a hurry. One of them was carrying a ballbat. I left the doorway, and huddled behind an old bedspring in a mound of garbage under the stoop. I could hear them shouting in Spanish and English: "Over here, Tony . . . You go over the fence . . . Anybody go up the roof? . . . Where's that broad?"

They went past me, and I came up from under the stoop, and hurried to Surf Avenue, hugging the walls. There was another doorway, beside an abandoned store at the corner, and I slithered into its dark cover. Now I could see Surf Avenue. About six young men were standing in front of the building, pointing in various directions. One of them was the Asp. Red Emma was no longer in front of the Half Moon Hotel. So I knew that Marta was all right. I didn't see any bodies and the Asp was walking around so she probably hadn't shot anybody.

Then I saw Red Emma coming down Surf Avenue. Marta must be cruising, I thought, looking for me. The young men saw her too. They ran into the middle of the street, as if prepared to block the car with their bodies. Some of them reached down and picked up bricks and bottles. Marta kept coming.

I ran out into Surf Avenue.

"Hey, you assholes!" I yelled. "Here I am!"

They turned, stopped for a moment, saw me standing a half block away, looked at the car, started for me.

I ran for the boardwalk. I ran with the bricks and rocks bouncing around me. I ran with everything I had left, pushing myself, my muscles bunching in my legs, a tear starting in my side. And they kept coming. I made it under the boardwalk, plunging into the sandy blackness. I ran past a sleeping wino. I ran past two young lovers nestling against a post. I ran around a heavy log. I could hear a thin whine in my chest. Still they kept coming. And still I ran.

I came out onto the beach at the base of the parachute ride. I hurried up the steps to the boardwalk. The rusting hulk of the old ride towered above me. I ran to a high wooden fence, hit it hard, scrambled up the fence, and dropped to the other side. I lay there, my heart pumping, my lungs ruined. I felt like giving up. Just lying there. Let them come. Let them beat me to death. Let them do what they wanted to do. I couldn't go anywhere any more. I couldn't move. I couldn't last another minute.

Then I heard their voices on the other side of the fence.

"Ice this muthafuck . . . Cool him right out . . . Get dis mutha, den cream the chick."

I held my breath, stood up, and moved to the ladder at the base of the old parachute ride. There was rubble everywhere. I found a piece of broken two-by-four and took it with me. Then I heard one of them hit the fence, try to leap it, and slide back down. I started up the iron ladder.

Then another hit the fence, made it to the top, and dropped over the side. There was no moon. I hoped they couldn't see me. I could climb fifty feet and wait them out. Another came over the fence and then another. I kept climbing. The wind was cold now off the ocean, and I shivered in the soaked suit. My shoeless feet were sore. The two-by-four felt greasy in my hand.

Then they spotted me. I saw them below me, pointing up. None of them seemed to have guns. One of them started up the ladder, and another up one of the pylons to my left. Then there were two more. I climbed higher. The wind whistled now. The old structure swayed gently. I could see all the lights of Brooklyn, the brightness in front of Nathan's, the arc of the Verrazzano, the distant glow of Manhattan. One of the young men was moving more quickly than the others, and a lot more quickly than I was. He was wearing a white zipper jacket, and coming at me, hand over hand. I was forty feet from the top. And I realized suddenly that they were going to get me. I might whack one of them with the two-by-four. I might kick one of them off. But they'd get me. If one of them had a gun, they were certain to get me.

The steel grids narrowed near the top, and there was a mushroom-shaped roof, where the parachutes used to stop and billow out, to slide down the long cables to the bottom. If I had to fight, I was better off staying where I was. There was more room. It was closer to the bottom.

So I wedged myself against a beam, and waited. The kid in the white shirt was almost on me. I looked down and saw the cold glint of a knife, as he came rung over rung, with the quickness and agility of youth.

And then I saw Red Emma.

Saw her pull up the street. Saw her stop on the street side of the wooden fence. Saw Marta get out. Saw her looking up past the fence to where I was.

The kid in the white shirt was three feet away. I swung the two-by-four and hit his arm but lost my club. It flew out of my greasy hands, clattering down through the steel superstructure. My weapon was gone. But so was his. He looked at his empty knife hand as if it belonged to a stranger.

And then I heard the first shot.

I looked down and saw Marta, holding the .45 with both hands, aiming it high. She fired again. From that distance, it sounded like the tiny snap of a rifle in a shooting gallery. The bullets clanged around the steel structure.

All the young men froze. Then one of them started down. I looked to my right, past one of the old cables, and saw another one start down. The kid without the knife waited. I pulled off my jacket and my shirt. I wrapped them together. Then I stood up, six feet over the kid, and started to inch, my way laterally across the beam, to the center of the structure. I leaned forward, wrapped the shirt and jacket around the old cable, grabbed tight, jumped, and started to slide back to the earth. Back to a place where I could walk. Back to Marta. I gripped the cable very tightly, so I would not move too quickly, but kept picking up speed. Then I wrapped my legs tightly on the old cable, and slowed down. I don't remember getting to the bottom. I don't remember getting out of Coney Island. I just remember that long ride down, and the distant shouting of the men above me, trapped in the bones of one of the skeletons of the lost paradise.

14.

I slept through the night and into the day, and woke up, and had soup, and slept again. Ike Roth would have to wait. They would all have to wait. I remember Marta telling me that she would stay with me until all of this was over, that she had taken a week's vacation, that I should sleep. And I remember the strangeness of being in a place where I didn't live, a place where the walls moved when I tried to focus on them, where the paintings were by painters she liked, not me, where the distant music was her music, not mine. I dreamed, but could remember nothing except a vague and continuous sense of dread. And when I woke up at last, it was night again. I was in Marta's apartment. And she was sitting across the room, looking at me in an amused way.

"Hello, dummy," she said.

"Hello, beautiful."

She was wearing a white shift and white sandals, sitting in a red chair. The Paul Davis poster for *The Cherry Orchard* climbed up the white wall behind her. The lights were muted. I was in her big bed, lying on crisp white sheets. Her skin looked very dark.

"Want to go to Coney Island for some hotdogs?" she said.

"There is no such place as Coney Island," I said. "It's a myth. It's a dream."

"You wish it were."

"How'd I get here?"

"United Parcel delivered you this afternoon," she said, stretching in the chair. "You arrived C.O.D. too. From some zoo."

"Ah well, at least I don't eat much."

"Not in the last twenty-four hours, you haven't."

I rubbed my chin. "Can I shave first?"

"Please don't."

"I've got things to do," I said. "I've got to go see a rabbi."

"Let him wait."

"The way he sounds, he doesn't let God wait."

"Want some breakfast?"

"No."

"How about some lunch then?"

"It's too dark in here for lunch."

"And dinner is out of the question, right?" she said, running the tip of her tongue over her lips.

"Of course."

"What do you want, then?"

"I want you to sit on my face," I said.

"Okay," she said, and reached behind her back, looking for the buttons.

Lee Avenue felt like the main drag of some small nineteenth-century Polish town. Marta stared out the window of the car in silence. Men in black caftan coats walked together arm in arm. Landau's Glatt Kosher Deli and Restaurant was still open, with kosher chickens roasting on a spit in the window. I pulled over, parked at a bus stop and went in. A few young Hasidim were sitting together at a table, drinking *Mayim Chaim*, the kosher soft drink. One of them was reading *Der Yid*. I asked the man at the cash register where the headquarters of the Marovicher Hasidim was. He gave me directions. I went back outside. Marta was out of the car, leaning on the fender. Three Hasidim walked past, and turned away, averting their eyes from her.

"It's so strange," she said.

"You can imagine what we must look like to them," I said.

"No, I can't," she said. "I can't imagine that at all."

We drove about four blocks along Lee Avenue, turned left a few blocks, then right again. The headquarters was an old four-story mansion, made of finely-meshed brick. There was a high picket fence, a gate, and a gravel path leading to the wooden door. Lights were burning on the first floor, but the upper stories were dark. I found a parking spot near the corner of the next block.

"You'll have to wait here," I said.

"Alone?"

"They're not too big on women," I said. "They won't let you in." I tapped the glove compartment. "The gun's in here, in case anybody comes around acting strange."

"I'm up to my ass in machos," she said.

"I'll try to make it quick."

I rang the gate bell four times before the door

to the house opened. I saw movement behind some of the venetian blinds, and then four Hasidim came out to the gate. One came forward and the other three held themselves ready a yard behind him.

"Yes," the first one said. "Can I help you?"

"I'm here to see Rabbi Kotz."

His face was puzzled. He spoke again, in cultured English: "Forgive me, but the hour is very late. Do you have an appointment with the *rebbe*?"

"No, but it's a very important matter. It's about a murder. A Jewish woman has been murdered. She was the wife of my cousin. One of the suspects is a Marovicher named Lev Pinchos. I come for guidance from the *rebbe*."

The young man's face turned ashen. He moved back to the others. They held a whispered conference. Then the first one came back. He took out a large iron key and opened the gate. It made a grating sound on the concrete path as he swung it open to let me pass. He locked the gate behind me. Then two of the others frisked me.

"Forgive these security measures," the first one said, as I was being patted down. "You must understand."

"To some degree, yes."

He started leading the way to the house. "I will speak to the *rebbe*. But I can guarantee nothing."

"Thank you."

"What is your name?"

"Briscoe. Sam Briscoe. I'm here about Lev Pinchos and Ike Roth. Ike Roth is my cousin."

At the door, each of them touched a *mezuzah*, the little scroll attached to the right doorpost, and then kissed their fingers. I did too, and followed them into a waiting area. There were posters in Hebrew, and a number of young men in side curls walking around in silence, reading The Book. The place was very clean, with hard parquet floors, white walls, dim lamps. There was a faint odor of stuffed cabbage. The three men who had come to the gate watched me carefully. I could hear prayers being mumbled somewhere in Hebrew. I remembered that year after my father died when I had been sent to live with my Uncle Moishe. My mother was ill then, although I didn't know why until years later, when she told me how she had cracked up after my father's death. Uncle Moishe was from the old country, and he tried teaching me Yiddish, and made me read the Pentateuch; he was big and rough and stern, a lifelong bachelor, who read the *Forward* every day, and translated the newspaper columns of someone named Singer for me and tried to get me to feel more like a Jew. I was ten years old and hated Saturday because I was forbidden on that day to write. I was writing every day then, letters to my mother in the hospital, stories of jungle boys and baseball players, of airline pilots and great heroes. I was even writing to my father. I knew he wasn't really dead. He was like Denny Colt in the comics, living in Wildwood Cemetery, coming out at night to become The Spirit, fighting all criminals and all enemies of America. After all, my father was a hero. How could he be dead?

"He will see you."

The young man was at my elbow. I hadn't heard him approach me, and I must have seemed alarmed.

"Oh," I said. "Oh, good. Yes. That's good."

He led me up a flight of stairs, along a narrow corridor and knocked gently on the door. A voice came from within, and the young man opened the door for me, and then faded away.

"Come in, Mr. Briscoe," the Reb Kotz said. "I used to read you all the time in the paper."

He was seated in an old-fashioned easy chair near a bay window. The room was large and spare. One bureau, a large bed. No rugs. No adornments. The room of an ascetic.

"Hello, rabbi," I said. "I've been reading about you too. For many years."

"You must think of me as a bit of a madman," he said in thickened English, smiling as I came closer. "You have always been such a radical in your printed work."

I smiled. "To be truthful, I wouldn't bring you an atomic bomb for your birthday. You might use it on City Hall, and I live a few blocks away."

He chuckled. He had a prayer shawl over his head and shoulders, and a gartel, a thin black cincture, draped on top of the shawl. He must have been praying when I arrived.

"You have a problem."

"Yes," I said. "It's about my cousin Ike Roth. And his partner, Lev Pinchos."

"Please be seated," he said, and motioned me to a chair in the bay, facing him. I could now see a part of the wall that was out of my sightline before. There was a lone photograph in a simple black Woolworth frame. From the distance, and at that angle, I couldn't make out the figures.

"It's a tragedy, of course, about Mrs. Roth," he said. "There is so much violence in this city. We know more than others. Every day we take the insults, the scorn, the spittle from hooligans. We fight back, but we can't fight everyone." He paused. "Did you know Ike Roth well?"

"He was my closest friend in the years when I was young," I said. "And in those days, he was a good man. A brave, generous man."

"Der mentsh iz vos er iz, ober nit vos er iz geven," he said. A man is what he is, not what he used to be.

"True," I said. "But I owe something to what he used to be. I'm going to try to find him. Before the police do. I think he's probably on the run and scared. I thought you might be of some help."

"Why me?"

"Because you knew him," I said. "And because you also know Monon Perez."

His eyes turned the color of cold rolled steel.

"What are you driving at?" he said testily.

"I mean that you might know why Ike was going to Puerto Rico. Who he was going to see there. And whether Monon Perez might have had Ike killed."

"I have never seen those men together," he said.

It was my turn for Yiddish proverbs.

"Des emes iz der bester lign," I said. The truth is the best lie.

He smiled. "Your Yiddish accent is terrible."

"Your English is an abomination."

"Ah," he said wearily, "another New York shtarker."

"When did you meet Monon?"

"In 1965. He had been a reformer. He picketed City Hall. He made scenes at the clubhouses of the Regular Democratic organizations. Somehow, he got one of the first poverty programs set up in the city. A small one. He continued to attack. But as we say in Yiddish, he who spits upward will have spittle on his face. Monon discovered quickly that he was spitting too high. He began to change. He began to accommodate."

"To cut everyone in."

"A living dog," he said, "is better than a dead lion."

The proverbs were now giving me a real pain in the ass; he was coming on like a road-company Khrushchev.

"When did he cut you in?" I said.

"The phrase is vulgar."

"The truth usually is."

"We wanted only to be treated fairly. My people work. They pay taxes like other citizens. But they don't use the city's schools, for which they pay taxes. They don't use the public hospitals, for which they pay taxes. They don't drive cars on the highways, for which tax money is used. But Monon saw that we voted. So he came to me. He sat in that very chair. He told me that he wanted to make certain we got our fair share. And we took our fair share. Nothing more. Nothing less."

"But you knew that he was a thief."

"I have no proof of that." He was very still now, staring at his thumbs.

"How did Ike Roth fit in?"

He leaned forward, his eyes fixed on the floor, as if groping for a way to explain something difficult.

"Did I say that Ike Roth fit in?"

"No," I said. "But he must."

He breathed out deeply. "Ike had handled some of our investments," he said. "We didn't like the way inflation was destroying our community's savings. Inflation was doing nothing to diamonds. Their value was, in fact, increasing. So Ike Roth did some investing for us. He was very good at it. We checked his work with some of our own people."

"Why didn't your own people do the investing?"

"Because Ike knew people we did not know," he said. "He was well connected with the Manhattan politicians. He knew the present governor in the Army."

"So you bought his political friendship by giving him some investment business, and a nice commission?"

"Again, your vulgarity—"

"His wife was murdered last night, rabbi. That was about as vulgar as you can get."

He rose slowly from his chair, his hands behind his back, as if closing the discussion. I rose with him, and circled around a few feet closer.

"Did you put Ike Roth together with Monon Perez?"

He nodded yes.

"Did you help bankroll Ike's partnership with Lev Pinchos?"

"Who is Lev Pinchos?"

"He's a member of your sect, rabbi. He certainly knows you."

"We might have invested some money in that firm," he said. "But investments are no crime. The earnings are put right back into this community. We do not spend money on fancy cars and fancy women. We—"

"I know that. But—"

I never finished the sentence. I was looking at the lone photograph on the wall. It was taken in a concentration camp. There were two men in the picture, standing behind the wire grid, wearing vertical striped uniforms, their shrunken bodies hidden, their faces like skulls. One of them was Mendel Kotz. The other was Lev Pinchos.

15.

He reached for the photograph and I chopped at his arms, and yanked it off the wall.

"I could make one shout and have you badly hurt," he said.

"*Az men ken nit baysn, zol men nit sh'tshiren mit di tseyn,*" I said. If you can't bite, don't show your teeth. "And pardon my fucking accent."

I looked at the two men. It must have been the last day of the war. It must have been on the same roll of film as the photograph in the office of Pinchos and Roth. I looked at Rabbi Kotz, and he seemed to be melting. He went back to his chair and sat down hard.

"All right," he said. "I'll tell you about it. The picture was taken on January 27, 1945. The day the Russians arrived. Everyone was sick. Outside our hut there was a great pit, filled to overflowing with corpses. We had been eating only potatoes for more than ten days. We had to get them from the earth, which was frozen like iron. We used pickaxes. That day, a Hungarian died picking at the earth. The Germans had already left, but we were all so sick we could not move. We watched planes fighting in the sky. We ate a cabbage soup one night. We tried to feel joy. Knowing the war was over, the Germans had left, the Russians were coming. But we felt nothing. We knew only that we had survived."

"You and Lev were together?" I said.

"We had each other," he said. "And we were both curious, Lev and I. We were curious about life. About what living must be like. Through everything, we insisted on staying alive to find out about living. When I was sick, he nursed me. When he was sick, I fed him. Near the end, when there was no bread, when our heads were shaved, nicked by the barber and then infected, when we all had lice, when the blankets were all gone, when the wooden shoes had been collected for the fires, we said no: We won't die. We will see New York. We will see Zion too. And we did. We did."

"You came here together?"

"In 1946. We were DP's. That photograph, and the one Lev has, those were our passports. They could not easily turn away two who had been in Auschwitz. We crossed the ocean in a crowded boat. We still smelled, or so we thought, of the camp, of the lager. A sweetish smell. Our hair had grown. We had gained weight. But we still remembered the stink of the crematoria at Birkenau. And we still smelled. That smell." He stared off at the blank wall. "Sometimes, late at night, when I am alone here, I think I smell it again, coming off me, coming from some part of my skin that has only been covered by new layers, and never replaced."

"And Lev? Why did he go to Israel? Why did he leave New York while you stayed?"

"There was a crime," he said. "In 1946, there was no work in New York, except what you made for yourself. The veterans were all home. The war industries were closing down. Lev spoke only Yiddish. No English, only some German he had picked up in the camp. And one night he borrowed a gun and held up a grocery store. For less than sixty dollars. He was caught a block away. I went the next morning to the courthouse and raised the bail. It was not much. The judge was a Jew, and I had that photograph. But Lev could not face prison. Not after what had happened. He fled to Canada, and from there back to Europe. I received only one letter from him. It was an apology, because he had jumped bail and he knew that I was poor. He said that he knew that our friendship was over. But that he was going to Palestine, and in Palestine he would fight. He would die fighting. He was certain of that. But he would never be the prisoner of any man again. I thought for certain that he must have died. And then, many years later, not long after the Yom Kippur War, he showed up again."

"Did the friendship survive?"

"No."

"That's too bad."

"He joined us. But he had changed. And I had become . . . well, whatever."

I put the photograph back on the wall.

"Did he try to sell you anything special in the past few months?" I said.

"Something special?"

"A piece of jewelry."

"No."

"He didn't hint that he had acquired a special piece?"

"No."

"Well, thank you, rabbi. I've got to go now."

"You can't stay for tea?"

"No."

He got up and walked me to the door. He seemed older than he was when I had arrived.

"Why do you have that picture on the wall?" I said. "Just that one lone picture."

"To remind me of when I was old," he said.

He stood at the door. I could hear the young men's voices, still praying down below. At the end of the hall, two of the bodyguards waited.

"Do you smell it?" he said suddenly. "Don't you smell it? Sweet, warm. Like death."

"No," I said. "I don't smell a thing."

Marta was dozing in the car, with the gun under her handbag, which was on her lap. I tapped the window on the driver's side and she whipped awake with the gun pointed at me.

"Open the door," I shouted. "Then shoot."

She relaxed and reached over and snapped the handle down to open the door, and I got in.

"Boy, you Hebes sure like to talk."

I put the car in gear and pulled out. "It's from drinking blood at ritual murders," I said. "You start talking for two people instead of one."

"How'd it go with the big macher?"

"Most of him I didn't like," I said. "But I respected him."

"Why?"

"He survived."

I headed back along Lee Avenue to the Williamsburg Bridge. All the shops were closed now. The street looked like some old country *shtetl*, before all the horror.

"Where we going?" she said brightly.

"To Puerto Rico," I said.

"Now?" she said, alarmed. "I don't have any clothes. I have to—"

"In the morning," I said. "First, we're gonna sleep together."

"Oh, goody," she said sarcastically.

"You know," I said, as we pulled onto the bridge, "I wasn't much of a Jew when I was a kid, and I'm even worse now. But basically, I was taught two things. Do unto others as you would have them do unto you. And don't fool around with *shiksas*." I reached over and took the gun out of her hand and slipped it into my pocket. "I'm beginning to think the second part was good advice."

"Kiss my ass," she said.

"I will," I said, as we came down the ramp onto Delancy Street. "I promise."

16.

    The loft seemed a place of almost luscious isolation. I parked Red Emma next to the kitchen, where the quarter-inch-thick sheet of acetate caught all the drippings, and went into the large, open main room, switching on lamps, while Marta headed for the kitchen. I put a record on the phonograph. Clifford Brown with strings, from some lost year in the fifties. Marta was quiet, as if she sensed that chat wasn't what I had in mind. I listened to the clear, beautiful tone of Clifford's trumpet, wishing in a vague way that he was still alive and that I could go up the next night and see him at Basin Street or Birdland and later drink whiskey with him and Max Roach. But Clifford was dead in a stupid accident and Birdland and Basin Street were gone and Max was teaching in a college somewhere and I wasn't going to be in New York tomorrow night and there were a lot of loose, jarring shards of fact and myth jamming against each other in my brain.

I called the service, as Marta threw coffee beans into the grinder and the beautiful smell of fresh-ground coffee mingled with Clifford's version of "Tenderly." Yes, there were messages. Charlie Kelly, the homicide cop; he would be at Clarke's. Jason Roth; could I be at the services for his mother? Malone, the cop; call when I came in. I called Jason. His voice was thick and groggy.

"Jason, it's Sam Briscoe."

"Oh, hello. Yeah, hello."

"Are you okay?"

"Yeah. I guess. It all happened so . . . I don't know."

"Is your sister there too?"

"Yeah. The doctor came over and gave her some sedation. We're at Frankie's house. He's a neighbor. They have this separate room, a private room, all that." He paused. "We buried Mom today."

"I'm sorry I couldn't come to the services, Jason," I said.

"I wish you had."

"I'm going to Puerto Rico on the first plane," I said. "I'm going to try to find your father."

Silence.

"Hello, Jason, you still there?"

"Yeah."

"Will you be okay?"

"I suppose."

"Listen, Jason, I'm sure your father is alive. And I'm going to bring him back."

"I don't think you can."

"Why not?"

"I think he's dead."

"What makes you think that?"

The young man hesitated. "I just . . . feel it. In my bones. So does my sister."

"Forget your bones," I said. "Get through this

next couple of days. And I'll call you from Puerto Rico."

"Where will you be down there?"

"Uh . . " I hadn't thought that far ahead. "The Caribe Hilton, probably. I'll call you if I go somewhere else."

He thanked me and hung up. I thought badly of myself for a moment; I should have abandoned Marta's bed and gone out there; I should have helped those kids through it. But they were dealing with the dead. I had to deal with people who were alive. Specifically, I had to deal with Ike Roth. And I was certain he was alive. For a moment, as Marta came out with the coffee, I thought about that piece of jewelry, and the thirty-three centuries it had been on the earth, and how a few more deaths were nothing in the bloody history that had accompanied its existence. How many Jews had been killed across those brutal centuries? How many more would die?

"Do you want some eggs?" Marta said quietly.

She looked beautiful in the muted light.

"No, the coffee will do," I said. "I need to clear my head."

"Of what?"

"Some boring Big Thoughts," I said. The coffee was hot and delicious. I called American Airlines and made reservations for the morning flight. Then I dialed some 800 area code and got the Hilton reservations people. They put me on hold, and I wondered where area code 800 was. Some terrible American limbo. A lost city, beneath the crust of the earth, inhabited by people from Avis and Hertz and American Express and Diners Club, an entire secret nation of reservations clerks and credit managers and telephone operators. Clifford finished playing, and I asked Marta to turn the record over, and then the operator came back and said yes, a room for two at the Caribe Hilton was confirmed and what flight was I on anyway? I told her and she thanked me in a dim, metallic voice and hung up.

"Time for bed, Sambo," Marta said. She sat on the deep plush couch against the stripped brick wall, under the drawing by Noel Sickles. "We have to get an early start. My place first, for some clothes."

"I've got credit cards," I said. "We can get some things down there."

"No way. Nobody pays for my rags but me." I dialed Clarke's. It was almost closing time, but Charlie Kelly was a late-shift man. The good homicide cops usually are. They took a while to find him. Finally he grunted into the phone:

"Yeah?"

"Sam Briscoe, Charlie."

"Ah, the Bad News Jew," he said.

"In person. Listen, I need to check something. This Fischetti who was shot in the Garden."

"Oh, yeah. The Knicks were trying to sign him, I heard. The Celtics got there first."

"Quit fucking around. You've been looking at it?"

"Possibly. Why?"

"Is this guy tied up with a character named Monon Perez, who runs a poverty racket over in Brooklyn?"

"Who told you that?"

"The fairy godmother."

"You have one of those in the family too?"

"Quit kidding, Charlie. It's important and I'm tired."

I heard him close the door of the booth.

"Yeah, they were connected at one time," he said. "This Perez was anxious to get a piece of the junk trade in his area. I don't know why. He had everything else, and most of it was clean. I mean, it was all clean on paper. I don't know how much stuck to his fingers."

"A lot."

"I don't know about that part of it. It's not my act. I just look at dead guys and try to figure who killed them. Anyway, Fischetti was a junk peddler out there in Brooklyn with a franchise from the Gambino operation. Gambino was a smart bastard. He saw the future was not in heroin. It was in real estate, in legitimate companies, in a lot of legal things. He had been encouraging his gunsels to start turning over the junk trade. Most of it went to the Cubans, and some to the P.R.'s. In Fischetti's area, that meant Perez. But Fischetti was a greedy bastard. He wasn't gonna turn it over without a legitimate deal in trade. So Perez cut him into the poverty money. As I get the story, it was a five-year deal. And it was up a few months ago."

"That makes Monon a pretty heavy suspect, right?"

"If Fischetti came around leaning on him hard, or threatening him, sure, Perez might figure it would be simpler to whack him out," Kelly said. "But he would have to get permission from the boys or they'd be burying a lot of Cubans and Puerto Ricans for the next month or two."

"Would they give permission?" I asked.

"They might, if they thought Fischetti was a pain in the ass," he said. "But I doubt it. It just wouldn't look right. All the young wise guys would get their olive oil up."

"That's racist, Charlie."

"I'm not a racist," he said. "I just don't like guineā wise guys." He laughed. "Hey, you're not writing any of this down are you?"

"Of course I am," I said. "For the *Ladies Home Journal*."

"What, you couldn't get it in *Colliers*? Or *Look*? Or the *Journal-American*?"

"I'll give them a call," I said.

"One other thing," Charlie said. I waited. "This Perez has a brother Nelson in San Juan."

"Yeah?"

"Yeah. And he's in the jewelry business."

"Jesus Christ."

"That's what I say," Charlie said, and hung up.

I sipped the coffee, but it was cold. Marta was dozing now on the couch, her long legs propped up on the pillows. I turned off the phonograph, and decided not to call Malone, the cop from Queens. He might tell me to meet him at the D.A.'s office. I rinsed the coffee cup and put out the lights in the kitchen and turned off the coffee brewer. Then I went back to Marta. I touched her arm and she was suddenly awake.

"Let's go to bed," I said.

"I thought you'd never ask."

17.

The flight to San Juan was full of kids. Kids in winter clothes and bright clean faces. Kids going home to see Grandma and Grandpa. Infants, held in the arms of young mothers, being brought home for ratification or approval. Kids who ran down the aisle and shouted at each other and bumped into stewardesses. It was always like that on the flight to San Juan. It had been like that for the twenty years I'd been going there, and it would probably be like that for twenty years more. I closed my eyes. Marta snuggled against me. I tried to doze but the kids kept running and shouting and falling.

It had been a morning of small hassles after a night that ended with teeth and lips and hair. Then in the morning it was the wait for the cab, because putting Red Emma in an airport parking lot was like sticking a sign on her saying "Please Steal"; the wait at Marta's house, as she packed clothes and left messages; the jammed traffic on the Fifty-ninth Street bridge, wondering where the hell all of them could be going, streaming the wrong way from Manhattan to Queens; last-minute calls at the airport, to Jason and Charlie Kelly; a stop at the Avis counter to reserve a car; checking in the rifle case, with my elaborate role as sportsman opening me to suspicion until I showed the various licenses; and then waiting on line, with the kids and their bright, appealing faces and their enormous energy for the production of noise. I tried to switch the tickets from tourist to first class to get away from the kids, but all the smart people had taken those seats, and we were stuck in this flying day-care center for the next four and a half hours.

"Try to sleep," Marta said.

"Not while the kiddies are playing stickball," I said.

"They're cute," she said, her clean-scrubbed hair smelling now of my shampoo.

"Like cobras," I said.

"Crank," she said, and tucked the pillow beside her neck and closed her eyes again.

I took a yellow pad from my briefcase and started writing down names hoping that just seeing them would force some connections. Lev Pinchos and Mendel Kotz. Ike and Sarah Roth. Ileana. Monon Perez and his brother Nelson Perez. Carmelo Fischetti. Auschwitz. The Mob. The Corso. It was all too scrambled. The only thing they had in common was that they were all in New York at one time, except for Nelson Perez. He ran a jewelry shop in San Juan. So I would have to check all the jewelry shops until I found him. I'd have to call all the hotels to see if Ike Roth had ever checked in. I'd have to check in with the Puerto Rican cops. Simon Sandino. I wrote his name down too. He was a

New York cop in the years when I was breaking into the newspaper business, but he couldn't crack the Irish Mafia in the department and went to San Juan, where he became a top homicide guy within a few years. I'd look him up. I'd call the San Juan *Star* and talk to Bob Friedman there, or Manny Suarez, and see what they had in the clips on Nelson Perez. I'd go out to the finca that Marta described, the one listed as owned by Carmen the wife, and see whether Monon was living in any of them. I read the clips I'd taken from the *Post*, but they were flat and stale and useless.

After a while, I slept.

I had been dreaming, full of deep, obscure dread, and then suddenly I was awake and a stewardess was nudging me and handing me a glass of orange juice. I looked at my watch. We were twenty minutes from San Juan.

"Almost home," Marta said. She was wide awake and looking fresh and young. I felt eighty-five years old.

"How come you look so great and I feel so lousy?"

"I lead a moral life," she said. "You are old and corrupt, unemployed and single. You pay for your sins, Briscoe."

"I guess I do."

"Don't be depressed," she said. "Redemption is always possible."

"I don't want to be redeemed," I said. "I want to give you a fast feel."

"Disgusting!" she said, and laughed, looking away at the great endless stretch of blue-green water.

We walked off the plane into the thick, humid air, and passed through a kind of revival meeting:

all the grandfathers and mothers and brothers and
sisters and uncles and aunts of all those kids were
at the gate. Squeals. Hugs. Tears. For a moment I
thought about my daughter, off in her mountain
school, skiing, speaking French; I wished I could
see her. And then we were turning around through
the lobby, following the streaming crowd, while
portable radios blared, and kids shouted, and we
found the baggage area. Marta waited for the
luggage while I went to the circular Avis counter
to get the car. Limo drivers were hustling the
new arrivals, offering cheap prices to go to mountain towns, to Ponce on the south side of the island,
to Mayaguez in the west. A few cops leaned against
a hurricane fence. The sky was very blue, and the
white concrete of the airport buildings looked like
salt in the sun. The Avis girl filled out forms,
looked at my Diners card and my driver's license,
again wrote laboriously, punched out some messages on the computer, searched in a drawer for
keys. I looked over at the baggage section, at the
milling, joyous crowd, and saw Marta coming
through with a porter. She was carrying the rifle
case herself. She looked very beautiful.

The reservation clerk at the Caribe Hilton asked
if I wanted a room in the new tower or a cabana on
the ocean and I told him I would take the cabana.
Then I said that I was expecting to meet a col-
league here, Mr. Isaac Roth. Had he checked in
yet? Roth? Roth? He punched some buttons, and
watched names play on a hidden screen.

No, sir, Mr. Roth has not checked in yet. He had
a reservation, uh, two days ago. But he didn't arrive,

and we canceled. Thank you. You're welcome, sir. Marta was silent through all of this. I took her hand, and we followed directions through the bar and out past the two swimming pools to the line of cabanas. The sun was scalding. Oiled bodies lay about, basting on mats and pool chairs, flattened into unconsciousness by the steady force of the sun. Kids played in the small pool near the cabanas. A young girl with large breasts only minimally encased in a bikini faced a young mustachioed man, the two of them bouncing a large rubber beach ball back and forth in the pool. Marta was silent. I held her hand. The bellman was waiting for us at the door. Off to the right, a bearded young walnut-colored Viking was explaining scuba diving to a group of very white visitors.

"Everything look good, right?" the bellman said, as we walked into the frigid air of the room. He opened the drapes and we could see the remains of Fort San Geronimo to the right, and a pathway, a sea wall, some rocks, and the sea.

"Yeah, everything looks good," I said, and slipped him five bucks. He smiled, handed me the key and left. Marta went to the back door and looked out through the glass at the sea.

"It sure is pretty," she said.

"That it is."

"You wonder why anyone ever leaves," she said. "Why anyone from here scrambles around New York, freezing and poor. I'd rather be warm and poor."

"They never think anything bad will happen to them," I said. "Like poor Sarah Roth."

She turned away from the door.

"Should we start working?"

"Yeah. They're a full day ahead of us," I said. "Whoever they are."

I pulled a San Juan telephone book from its slot under the phone in the night table.

"Start with the hotels," I said. "See if Ike Roth has checked into them. Try some of those cheap guest houses out in Isla Verde. I don't think he'd be dumb enough to use his own name, but we've got to be sure."

"What are you gonna do?" she said.

"Unpack," I said, in a chilly way.

She walked away from the window, and picked up the phone book. I threw the first suitcase on the bed and started to empty the clothes.

Two hours later, she had finished calling every hotel and guest house in San Juan, and Ike Roth hadn't registered at any of them. It was a waste of time, but it had to be done. At each place, she had asked whether Mr. Roth had checked in yet. When she was told he hadn't, she said to please leave word for him to call Mr. Briscoe as soon as he arrived from New York. If Ike did register in any of these places in the next few days, he would have a message waiting for him. While she did all that, I took the shoulder holster out of my suitcase, and the Colt out of the gun case. I put in a fresh clip, and left out three more clips. I'd also brought a Wichita classic rifle and an old 12-gauge Parker shotgun with 28-inch barrels. I didn't think I would have to use the long guns, but they did make me look like one of those New York dudes who come down to rent a cabin cruiser and shoot at sharks. I left them in the case and stood the case in the closet.

When Marta finished one of her calls, I ordered lunch from room service.

"Where'd you get all the hardware?" she said.

"I bought the forty-five," I said. "The other two were gifts."

"From who?"

"Loan companies," I said. "They wanted to make it an even contest when they came around to break my legs."

"Have you ever used any of them?"

"Yeah," I said, but I didn't elaborate, and she didn't press me.

Lunch arrived: fruit salads and a platter of seafood and some iced tea. I signed and added a tip, and the man from room service went away. I took everything out the back door to the little porch with its table and two chairs. The afternoon was very hot, a warm breeze blowing off the sea.

"You look strange when you handle guns," she said, sipping her iced tea.

"Everybody does," I said. "You looked strange in Coney Island. Especially to the bad guys."

She looked out to sea, where whitecaps were breaking in the distance.

"Did you ever go hunting with your father?"

"No. He died when I was ten," I said.

"What . . . what happened?"

"He was shot in a cheap holdup in Brownsville," I said. "He was a cop. And he was off-duty, having a drink in a saloon on Livonia Avenue late one night, when three stick-up men came in. He took them on. He killed two of them, but the third guy got a shot off on the way out the door and killed him."

"My God."

"God had nothing to do with it," I said, and finished my shrimp.

I got up and went inside and called Simon Sandino at police headquarters in Rio Piedras. I had been there once, when Simon took me on the grand tour. It was a huge, windowless cube built to survive an atomic explosion. Simon was riding high in those days, the brightest detective in the division, fighting for modern equipment, developing his own network of stool pigeons and other specialists, using the techniques of New York street cops in his own home town. He was married to a strawberry blonde from Ponce, the daughter of some old, respectable family from that stuffy colonial town, and she had carried the town with her to San Juan. She filled thier house with heavy furniture, sets of polished silver, woven tapestries, Persian rugs, leather-bound books, and pictures of Madrid. My wife liked her; they talked about jewelry and servants and dinner parties; but Simon never seemed comfortable with her. He was only happy putting bad guys in jail.

"Detective Sandino? *Quiere* Detective Sandino?"

"Si, senor."

"Detective Sandino? *Quiere* Detective Sandino?" and then he came back. "*Tengo un numero aqui*," he said, and gave me a number, and hung up quickly. I dialed the number. It was the Bayamon substation, out in the suburbs. I asked for Detective Sandino, and was told to hold on, and then heard the familiar voice.

"*Bueno?*"

"Simon? It's Sam Briscoe."

"You're kidding! Where are ya?"

"The Caribe, with the tourists and the flamingoes."

"Son of a bitch," he said. "It's been, what? Four years?"

"Almost five."

"Well, get your ass out here!"

"What are you doing in Bayamon?" I said. "Isn't that the Puerto Rican Staten Island?"

"Hey, you know how it goes, Sam," he said sadly. "There was an election. The new party won. Suddenly I was the old guard, I was suspect, they wanted me out of there and one of their own guys in. They couldn't fire me. But they could reassign me. So here I am."

"That's too bad."

"Hey, come on out."

"I will, Simon," I said. "But I'd like a favor. Have someone check the hospitals and the morgue for a man named Isaac, or Ike Roth. He's my cousin. He's about five-ten, a hundred and seventy, thinning hair, good teeth."

There was a pause as he wrote down the details.

"What's it about, Sam?" he said.

"I'll tell you when I see you," I said. "But two days ago he was alive."

"You think he's dead?"

"He might be."

He paused. I could hear someone talking to him in the station house, and Simon half-covering the phone and shouting back. He laughed and came back to me.

"You alone?" he said.

"No, I've got a friend with me."

151

"You usually do."

"What about you, Simon? How's the wife?"

"What wife?"

"Ah well," I said.

"She wanted me to go to goddamned novena and join some goddamned country club with all the statehood crowd," he said. "I just wanted to drink and screw. Especially, I wanted to screw her, but she found it vulgar. She believed in virginity, both before and after marriage."

I laughed.

"It's okay," he said. "She married a guy from the party that won."

He laughed and so did I, and I told him I'd call him before driving out to Bayamon.

"Who's that?" Marta said, coming in from the porch. The sea was pounding now, the tide chewing at the beach.

"Simon Sandino," I said coldly. "He's a good cop." I exhaled hard. "All right, let's start checking the jewelry shops."

In that moment, I hated my voice and my manner and the way I was treating Marta. She had saved my life. She had risked her own. She had packed a bag and come with me to this place, which was her home country, and should be beautiful to her, and there might be someone else out there among the palm trees waiting to kill the both of us. And something mean was running through me, like a large chilly wind, and I was taking it out on her with coldness and efficiency. The truth was that there was another reason why I didn't want to be in Puerto Rico, but I couldn't think of a way to tell Marta Torres why. I couldn't tell her what it was like that first winter with my wife, freshly married and loving each other, when we came here and made love on a high floor of this hotel and danced late in its night club and made love later on the sand, like a scene out of "From Here to Eternity." I could talk about it with Marta, I could make words come out of my mouth, but I knew I would lie and give myself all the best lines. That's why I was a writer. I would crack wise and make it sound worse than it really was, and thus try to diminish what it once meant to me, and Marta would believe me, and that would be the worst thing of all.

So instead of talking, I lifted the San Juan phone book and sat on the edge of the bed; wishing that none of this had happened, that Ike had never met Lev Pinchos, that I hadn't seen Ike at the Garden, that those two kids in Israel had gone somewhere else to dig that morning and that the goddamned breastplate of Aaron had remained in its sandy tomb. My head hurt; my face felt pulpy from the fists of the Turtle; and I could feel the meanness shifting, like a raft in a tide, and it was turning now into violence and I wanted to kill someone. I wanted to break faces and bones. I wanted to shoot holes through someone. I wanted something definitive and final to happen, so all of this would be over, and I could go somewhere with Marta where I was not imprisoned by duty or history.

There was no Nelson Perez listed in the phone book, no Perez Jewelers, not even a San Juan Jewelers Association where we might check the membership. I called the San Juan *Star*; after a two-minute wait, the operator put me through to Bob Friedman. I asked him to check the clips on Nelson Perez for me and he said he would, but that he was on deadline and would call me back in forty-five minutes. He was a good reporter and a nice man and for years he had been a stringer for the *Daily News* in New York. When he said he would call in forty-five minutes, I knew it would be forty-five minutes. I hung up and looked at Marta.

She was wearing tight maroon slacks and a white shirt that made her skin look golden. She leaned against the closet, sleek and rounded and strong, with that flawless golden skin and the ripe breasts and belly and the lean, strong legs and that lithe narrowness of waist. She was staring at me, in an uncertain, puzzled way.

"I'm sorry I'm such a mean bastard."

"It's okay," she said.

"No, it's not."

She came over and sat beside me on the bed. "Do you want to talk about it?" she said.

"I can't," I said.

"Is it Ike?" she said. "Are you afraid for him?"

"I wish I hadn't lost that day after the Turtle," I said. "But no, it's not Ike."

She touched the back of my neck, and ran cool fingers along the edges of the bandage.

"You've been beaten up twice in two days," she said. "People tried to kill you. Your cousin's wife is dead and your cousin is missing and their two kids might be orphans. You've got a right to feel shitty."

"But I've got no right to make you feel shitty too."

She smiled. "You Jews do horde the guilt, don't you?"

I squeezed her hand. "Just most of the world's supply."

"Why don't you let me decide whether you're making me feel rotten," she said. "Just for your information, Sambo, I feel nothing of the kind."

"Thanks," I said. She put her arm around me, and held me.

"Why don't you just nap for half an hour?" she said.

I lay back, and she lay beside me, with her feet on the floor.

"When you feel like talking about the other things," she said, "please make an appointment."

"Thank you, Dr. Torres."

"And for you, there's no fee."

18.

Forty-one minutes later, Friedman called. Marta sighed. I grabbed a pencil and started writing. Nelson Perez. Big in Cuban community of about 8,000. Ran dinner-dance for group called Puerto Rico for Nixon in 1968. Once hosted dinner for Somoza, dictator of Nicaragua. Brought boatload of Cuban refugees into San Juan harbor on fishing boat in 1969. Catholic, but has connections with Evangelical Christians. Supported campaigns against abortion, women's rights, and gun control. Investments in Miami. Runs jewelry chain called "Gems of the World." One big shop in Old San Juan, on Calle Cristo. Another in the Hato Rey shopping center, smaller, a branch. Two more in Miami. Signed full-page ads opposed to Panama Canal treaties. Also part of group that closed down San Juan *Review* for being "too left-wing." They did it by drying up all advertising. There was nothing about a brother in New York. Particularly a Puerto Rican brother.

"Christ, Bob, it's almost a cartoon," I said.

"He's your typical Mark One All-Purpose Cuban

Exile, all right," he said. "Hey, what's this about?"

"I don't know yet," I said. "If it's anything good, I'll give it to you first."

"Great."

"I'll see you, Bob."

"Just watch your ass. Some of those people are a little nuts."

"I know," I said. "Take care."

I got up and washed my face. Marta followed me into the bathroom.

"You're a hairy bastard," she said, running a fingernail down my back.

"Yeah. That's why it's vanishing on my head. When the lanolin gets through feeding my chest and my legs, there's nothing left for the top of the balloon."

I strapped on the shoulder holster.

"Let me rub you for luck," she said.

"Control your lust, will you, woman?"

I called Simon Sandino. He said there was no Ike Roth in the hospitals or the morgue. No Americans. Not even an aging hippie leaking heroin. I told him I would call him later at home. He gave me the number, and I wrote it on an index card and slipped it into my back pocket. I pulled on a brown-checked lightweight jacket that hung loosely over the holster. Then I put the .45 into the holster.

"Ah, the well-dressed hit man goes for a ride," Marta said.

"I hope I don't have to use the goddamned thing. It makes so much noise and such big holes. Here. These are extra clips. Keep them in your purse."

"You expecting to meet an army or something?"

"No, I'm just not as good a shot as you are."

I took the rifle case out of the closet, pulled on

a golf cap, masked myself with sunglasses, and locked the front and back doors. Marta was smiling and for the first time all day I felt like a human being.

We walked across the parched grass that separated the swimming pools. The kids were all going home. A few stewardesses huddled together in the last precious rectangle of sun. We had to go through the bar to get to the lobby. There was an ass on every stool and so many tall colored drinks on the counter it looked like a soda fountain. A syrupy salsa version of "By the Time I Get to Phoenix" was playing on the sound system. A couple of hungry-eyed middle-aged women watched us from a table on the terrace, their faces shining with alimony tans. As we walked by, Marta rolled her hips a little harder than usual.

"You must have been something when you were fifteen," I said as we walked into the lobby.

"At fifteen I was flat-chested," she said. "At sixteen my father made me stop wearing T-shirts. It was all so sad. I couldn't play ball with the boys anymore."

"They must have killed themselves en masse."

"No, they just started stealing cars instead, and trying to get me and my girl friends into them."

"Did you go?"

"None of your business."

We took the car out of the lot, and I swung right, past Sixto Escobar Park, where I had watched Jose Torres box a draw with Benny Paret one hot night, twenty years earlier, and then went along the cliff road beside the ocean to Old San Juan. The Commonwealth government buildings were along the left, huge piles of architectural rhetoric built to make a colony feel as if it were truly self-governing; they had succeeded only in making most of the occupants feel puny. Off to the right was the sea, the rollers piling in from the South Atlantic, which looked wide and dark and savagely beautiful in the fading light.

"Won't all these joints be closed?" Marta said.

"No. The department stores, yes. The stationery stores, probably. The book stores, of course. But the cruise ships are in. I saw them from the plane. And when the cruise ships are in, the jewelry stores stay open."

"They sure couldn't sell most of that junk to Puerto Ricans."

"They can barely sell it to the cruise ships," I said.

I turned left at the Plaza Colon, where a few lone Puerto Rican women were sitting on benches, waiting for buses, with shopping bags at their feet. A few kids lolled under the plane trees, but there weren't many other people around. The old Puerto Rican families were all gone from San Juan now, except for those who lived in the green tar-papered shacks of the slum called La Perla, over the hill to the right, beyond the walls of the old fortress. The place had become chic. It had been taken up. Aggressive young mainland-educated couples lived here now, caught up in pop art and independence movements and their subscriptions to *New York Magazine*. American businessmen lived here. A fairly large community of gays lived here. A handful of retired CIA agents lived here, dreaming of the bad old days, sworn to eternal silence. But there were not many ordinary Puerto Ricans anymore. Certainly nobody who was poor.

I drove around behind the Tapia Theater, and up Recinto street. To the left, the cruise ships rose from their moorings, huge and white, flying Norwegian flags, Greek flags, British flags. They did not come from Conrad's ocean, or Melville's; these were seagoing hotels, full of people who had waited too long to see what lay around them on the earth, and were trying hard now to buy back those lost young years. What they really wanted, they couldn't buy. A few small clusters of them were crossing the street, as we pulled into a parking spot in front of the Escorial Book Shop. None of them seemed to know each other and they all walked as if their feet hurt. One heavy blonde woman with lobster-colored legs had smeared a thick paste of Noxzema over her nose; she looked like Cyrano in drag. I wondered about all their dreams.

The side streets were still full of people as we walked up the hill to Calle Cristo. Women without shoes carried naked babies and worked the tourists for a few quarters' worth of pity. Merengue music pounded out of one of the local bars, and a few old men sold lottery tickets; the tourists did not buy lottery tickets because they were never coming back. In the square on Calle San Francisco two middle-aged men watched the public television set where, years before, I had watched a kid named Cassius Clay beat Sonny Liston for the heavyweight championship of the world. That year, the square was jammed, and they roared in delight as the brilliant boy danced and stabbed at the hulking bear. Now everybody had their own TV sets and the audience in the square had gone off somewhere and Liston was dead and Clay had become Ali, and couldn't fight much anymore.

"Someday, I want to take you to a place I've never been," I said, as we moved up the hill toward the Fortaleza, where the reigning governor lived.

"As long as it's warm," Marta said.

Then we saw it. Gems of the World. The store filled an entire building on the corner of Calle Cristo, and it had been decorated in the usual boutique good taste. Such taste did not grow from use or history; it was mechanically applied, like spray paint. So the name of the store did not scream in neon; it was chiseled onto bronze plaques to make you feel you were in the presence of dignity and class. The outside walls were whitewashed, the balcony woodwork stripped of old paint, stained and varnished to evoke the nineteenth century. The goods in the windows glittered in spare, classical settings.

"Well, it doesn't look like Irv's Fourteenth Street Cut-rate Jools," Marta said.

"In some way," I said, "it looks worse. This is the come-on. So come on: Let's play sucker."

We went in together, Marta holding my arm. A few dozen tourists moved around glass-topped tables, inspecting the goodies, attended by a number of salesmen in ties, and women in long hostess dresses. One of the women darted away from the group, like a barracuda sighting a wounded child. She was on the heavy side, her body covered with a bright multicolored muu muu. Her hair was rinsed blue. She was wearing rouge. She spoke English with a Bronx accent.

"Welcome to Gems of the World," she said, as if cassette number twenty-three had just been pressed in her brain. "I'm Irma. I'm here to help.

Not to sell. Just to help. We try to get the customer's preferences. We try to help the customer understand the tremendous variety of gold and jewelry and get the best price for his or her needs. We—"

"What do you have in wedding rings?" I said.

"Well, well, well," she said, eyeing Marta and freezing the smile on her face. "Isn't that wonderful!"

"Something in gold," I said.

"One ring or two?" Irma said.

"Three," Marta said.

"Yes, we want the baby to have a ring too."

The woman's smile broadened, but her eyes were puzzled. "What a wonderful idea!"

"The baby's only four months old," Marta said, "so you'd better show us a small one. And for my man here, I want the nose kind."

"The nose kind?"

"You know," she said, not blinking, "the kind you put in the nose."

"Well, I don't . . . Are you putting me on?"

"Actually, no," I said. "But I do want to see your chastity belts while I'm here. Something in silver, with emeralds maybe. I've gotta go out of town for a few days."

"Oh, for goodness sakes, Sam. Emeralds wouldn't match my color! Rubies. It has got to be rubies."

"Whatever you say, sweetheart," I said, smiling at Irma. "Make it rubies. What the hell. You only get married twice."

She turned away from us and waved at a thin young mustachioed man with a face like a hatchet.

"George? Would you talk to these people?"

George must have been the security man. Or the

guy who handled trouble. Or both. He came over
with his right hand in his pocket, like he'd seen a
lot of George Raft movies.

"Can I help you?"

"Yeah. I want to see Nelson Perez."

He looked me over. "I don't know if Mr. Perez
is still here."

"Tell him it's about a murder, George."

George didn't blink.

"Tell him Ike Roth's cousin is here, George."

"I doubt if he's still here."

"You call him, George. You tell him to come
down here, George, because I want to talk to him.
Real bad."

I was doing Bogart to his Raft, and it seemed to
work. He walked to the back of the store, and
picked up a wall phone. He watched me as he
talked. Then he came back.

"Mr. Perez said that he is just finishing with a
customer," George said. "He said to make yourself comfortable. He said he should not be long.
Can I bring you and your . . . friend a coffee or a
drink?"

"No thanks, George. We'll just sit here and watch
the natives dance by in the street."

George went back to his location, glued to a
wall beside a giant tin copy of the Aztec calendar
stone. Marta and I sat on a rattan couch. It was
warm now, the air close. Traffic moved slowly
along the cobblestoned path. Irma pinched at her
muu muu, which was sticking to her body, and
busied herself with a nice older couple in Somerset
Maugham clothes. They looked as if they might be
in the market for a silver-plated ceiling fan, that
could beat the air like it was batter while Sadie

Thompson played her phonograph in the rainy upstairs room. Marta smoked. A half hour went by.

Then a squat man in a tan suit came out of the
back of the store. He looked like a squashed version
of Monon Perez; he was shorter, fatter, and grayer,
with a mustache that was trimmed to look
distinguished, and looked instead as if it had been
borrowed from an actor. He came straight to us.
He didn't offer a hand.

"Yes?" he said, peering at me with gray steady
eyes. His lips were very dry.

"I want to talk to you about Ike Roth," I said.

"Who?" He wet his lips and tried to design his
face into a pattern of innocence.

"Listen, Nelson, we can jerk off or we can talk.
Let's not jerk off."

"Ike Roth . . . Hmm. I seem to recall that name.
Is he a gem salesman?"

"You know who he is. You've done business with
him. He came down to see you two days ago. With
something very special. You had lined up a big
customer for him. Maybe you were the special customer. But who knows? The cops will have to
figure that one out."

"Are you with the police?"

"No," I said. "I'm Ike's cousin. I told George
that. Your errand boy over there."

"I haven't seen Mr. Roth," he said, in formal
English. "He did say something about coming down
here. But in this business, people are always vague
about dates and departures. If others know when
you are coming, and what you are carrying, it can
be a great temptation."

He looked around the room for a moment, seeing
potential thieves and traitors everywhere, disguised

as salesmen and customers and pedestrians in the street. "A great temptation," he said. "These days, people think nothing of breaking the law. The old traditions are gone. The old pride. The old belief in the nobility of service."

"Cut the speech, Nelson," I said. "I've heard that stuff at every Chamber of Commerce meeting I've ever gone to, and it doesn't improve with use."

"It's true, however . . ."

"No, I don't think it's the people who work for you that do the stealing," I said. "In my experience, most stealing is done by the people who become bosses. They steal cities. Countries. Whole governments."

He tried a cold, hard look on me, and then turned to go.

"Excuse me," he said, "I have an important call to make."

I grabbed his forearm and squeezed hard.

"Just a minute, pal," I said.

George came over quickly, his hand sliding inside his jacket. I dug my nails deeper into Nelson's arm and whispered to George:

"If you take that rod out, junior, I'll shove it up your ass."

"George, please wait over there," Nelson said.

George looked at me as if he'd already cut my throat but he obeyed. "Please release my arm," Nelson said. "Please don't make a scene in my place of business."

"I want to talk to you about something that used to belong to a man named Aaron."

I let go of his forearm, and I thought he would fall. His face grew pasty and soft.

"Aaron who?"

"The first one," I said. "He didn't have a last name. He died thirty-three centuries ago."

"I . . . don't know what you're talking about."

"Yes, you do."

"I barely know Ike Roth. I bought a few things from him. Cheap things. A few sights of industrial diamonds, which I sold in bulk to some commercial firms here."

"Did a fella named Carmelo Fischetti come down here with Ike?" I said. "You know good old Carmelo. He died suddenly the other night in Madison Square Garden. A bad pain in the chest. And what about your brother Monon? Was he with Ike on any of those trips?"

His color was gone now. He looked sick and trapped.

"Do you want to tell me the story?" I said. "You can tell it to me, or you can tell it to the cops. It might be easier with me."

He glanced at his watch. There were fewer tourists in the place now. George stood dutifully at his station. Irma was walking to the back, flapping her muu muu as if to cool off her sweating thighs.

"Come with me," Nelson said.

We followed him to a small elevator in the back and went up with him and into an office. Heavy golden drapes covered the windows. An air conditioner purred below the drape line to the right. Nelson moved around behind his desk. The wall was covered with pictures: Nelson and Nixon, Nelson and Bebe Rebozo, Nelson and Jerry Ford, Nelson and Barry Goldwater, and Nelson and Nelson—Rockefeller, that is. They all grinned in the foolish way that people grin when they are faking friendship for a camera. His desk was bare, except for a decorative jeweler's scale, with two perfectly balanced pans suspended on chains.

"I should tell you something," I said, as I sat down facing him. Marta sat on a couch at an angle to the wall. Everything was decorated in executive leather. "I've got a gun. And if I have to, I'll use it. So don't do anything stupid."

"Of course not."

"Just tell the story."

He leaned forward on the desk and stared at his thick hands. His fingers were very white and even, like tubes. The fingernails were highly polished.

"It began in Israel," he said. "Almost a year ago. I go to Israel often. A great nation. Great leadership. And along with Antwerp and New York, one of the most important cities in the gem business. I was at a cocktail party in my hotel in Tel Aviv, when I was approached by a young man. He had a patch on one eye, like a young Moshe Dayan. And he told me a story about this . . . about the breastplate of Aaron. He said that it had been discovered again, after many centuries, by a friend of his. And then it had been stolen. The young man knew that I did a great bulk business. That I had contacts in all of the diamond centers and in America. He thought perhaps this piece had found its way to America. And he wanted me to look for it."

"For who?"

"For someone who could pay a very large sum to have it returned," he said. "He didn't mention then who it was. But he said he was contacting some dealers and asking them to please look out for the piece. I told him that I would try, and immediately forgot the whole thing. People always ask strange things at cocktail parties, and this was just another strange thing. Do you mind if I have a drink?"

"It's your office."

He got up and his short legs carried him to a tall cabinet. He took out a bottle of dark Bacardi rum and gestured at Marta and me to see if we wanted drinks. We both shook our heads no. He poured an inch of rum and took a single cube from an ice bucket and plopped it into the drink.

"Then a month ago, my brother called me from New York," he said. "We are not close. I don't like some of the people he deals with. His style is not my style. He called to say that a man we both knew had a strange piece of jewelry to sell. It was very old, very rare, with Jewish markings on it."

"The man was Ike Roth, of course."

"Of course," he said sipping the rum. He looked at the wall. He looked at Marta. He looked at the drink.

"And Ike was a fence," I said, really winging it now. "He had brought you hot diamonds and jewels before, things that had been recut, or remounted by his partner, Lev Pinchos. You had done handsomely with things from Ike Roth before. So you listened hard when you heard his name." He was staring hard at me now. "That's the way it went, isn't it?"

He whispered. "Close."

"Did he bring the piece here?"

"No. I didn't know for sure what it was. I didn't know whether it was a stolen archaeological piece, or a piece that could even be legitimately sold. But I knew Roth."

"Why didn't he call you personally?"

"I think he was afraid of the so-called normal channels," he said. "Even . . . even the underground markets have their rules. But my brother was friendly with various other people. Rabbis in New York who might be interested. Others. I asked Monon for color photographs, and a few days later he sent me some slides. The piece looked extraordinary. But it was nothing to cut up for wedding rings. I remembered clearly that young man with the eye patch from Tel Aviv. I wrote him a brief note, saying only that I had reason to believe that the piece he was looking for had surfaced in New York."

"What was his name?"

"Ira Goldstein, I believe. I sent the letter. Four days later he called me from Antwerp. He asked me many questions, including the name of the New York dealer. He implied that he was working for the Israeli government, but he sounded obsessed. Finally, to get rid of him, I gave him Ike Roth's name. The same day my brother Monon called. I told him what I had done. He was furious. He told me to call this Goldstein in Antwerp and tell him to forget Ike Roth, that other plans had been made. I did. And that was all I heard until today."

"What did you hear today?"

"That Ike Roth's wife was dead."

"How did you hear that?"

"A policeman called me from New York. His name was, I believe, Malone."

I got up. He sipped his drink. "Where's your brother now?"

"I don't know."

"And what about Carmelo Fischetti. Do you know him?"

"I did. Years ago. Right after the fall of Cuba. I met him briefly in New York. He was just another stupid killer. I had nothing to do with him. But yes, he did come here with Ike Roth on the last trip, two months ago. I suspected that Ike was helping him sell some . . . jewelry. He remembered me. I did not remember him. He reminded me of the circumstances, which were not pleasant. Before he left, he bought some cuff links downstairs. He wanted a discount. I gave it to him."

I was starting to like Nelson Perez. That kind of detail could not be a lie.

"Let me ask you something personal," I said. He waited for the question, his eyes guarded, but more lively now from the rum. "Explain this elaborate goddamned masquerade about you being a Cuban."

He smiled for the first time, looking like the ingratiating man who always runs the Latino section in a political campaign. "Ah, *that*. Well, it's simple. When I was young, there was nothing for me in Puerto Rico. I went to Cuba, to make my way there. I went for a summer, and stayed fourteen years. I ended up running a jewelry shop in the Hotel Nacional in Havana, and I was doing well. Then came Castro and I had to come here. My accent had become Cuban. Many of my friends were Cuban." He cleared his throat. "And at that time, it was useful to be a Cuban. There was money around, to help Cubans."

"CIA money."

"I didn't ask too many questions about where it came from. I took it, and started over."

"Did Monon work for you?"

"Only for a while. As I said, I didn't like him very much. We had grown up differently, he in Puerto Rico, I in Cuba. But he was my brother, and I helped him get started in New York."

"In the poverty racket?"

"I made a few calls to Washington," he said in a soft voice. "I hoped he would stay in New York. He didn't. He bought property here, in the south. He came to get deals on jewelry. He did not stay away." He made a hapless little move with his free hand. *"Eso es la vida."*

His voice trailed off. I nodded at Marta, and she got up, looking at Nelson.

"What happens now?" Nelson said.

"We'll know soon."

I started to go out. Then something pushed through the broken circuits of my brain. A name. A memory. A piece of a conversation with Lev Pinchos.

"The name of the buyer in Israel. You said that your contact—the man with the eye patch—didn't tell you the buyer's name that first time in Antwerp. Did he tell you the name when you spoke on the phone last month?"

"Yes, he did."

"Was that name Rebecca?"

His eyebrows arched in surprise. "Why, yes. Rebecca. That was the name. Rebecca Kovner, I believe."

"Thank you, Nelson, and good night."

19.

I grabbed Marta's hand when we were safely out the door, and we hurried around the corner. My mind was racing hard. Marta wanted to know what Nelson was talking about: the thing that belonged to Aaron, and all the rest. I tried to explain it all. I told her what Lev Pinchos had told me, about the girl named Rebecca and her boyfriend Arieh who had found the piece in the dig on the West Bank. I apologized for not telling her all of it before, and tried to explain why: that I didn't want strangers trying to kill her to find out what she knew. She smoldered for half a block, but I was already knitting the pieces together. On Calle Tetuan, I stepped into a restaurant and found the pay phone and called Simon Sandino's home number.

"Hey, where the hell you been?" he said. "I've been trying to find you."

"I need some more help, Simon."

"First let me tell you what's up."

"Shoot."

"About ten minutes ago, I got a call from headquarters," he said. "Some *jibaro* kids were playing in the hills behind the rain forest. They found a body. It was completely burned, and apparently had been shot. They say it's an American."

"Goddamn it."

"I've got nothing else on it. But I'll go out there with you if you want."

I was too late. I'd blown it. They'd grabbed Ike, got the piece from him, taken him out on some road, and killed him.

"Shit," I said again. "Shit. Shit."

Simon's voice dropped a bit. "You'd better get out here fast," he said. "The headquarters guys have the case and they'll screw it up for sure."

"I'm on my way," I said. "Meanwhile, you got any guys at your place who can make some calls for me?"

"A few. They're covering stolen bicycles and exciting things like that. But I think I can spring them."

"Okay. Have them check all the airlines for the past few days. Look at the manifests. See if a woman named Rebecca Kovner arrived here in the past few days. She must be in her twenties. Traveling on an Israeli passport. She might have a few more people with her, so see if there were any other Israelis on the planes. Try the name Ira Goldstein."

He said he would try to get the information, and then gave me the directions to the substation in Bayamon, where he would meet us. I hung up and stepped out of the booth.

"Want me to go back and start checking hotels for this dame?" Marta said.

"No, you better come with me."

173

"Afraid itsy-bitsy li'l me will get hurt?"

"The truth? Yeah."

We stepped out into the warm night. In an upstairs room, I could see two middle-aged men sitting in opposite windows of a tastefully decorated apartment. The balcony doors were open to the night. One of the men fingered a violet foulard. Sabicas was playing on the phonograph. They did not move.

Simon Sandino had put on weight. His oval, teak-colored face was round now, and the hard stomach had become a belly. But he glowed excitedly as we walked into the one-story blue police building a block off the Bayamon road. There were maps of the town on the wall, and a picture of the new governor and the President of the United States, and some WANTED pictures in Spanish, and some photographs of missing teenage girls. A young woman in a police uniform was behind the desk. Her heavy-breasted body was crumpling the starch in her shirt.

"Hey, it's good to see you, man," he said, giving me a warm abrazo. "How's things in El Bronx?"

"The last time I looked, there was a lot less of it."

I introduced him to Marta and he was formal and flirtatious, and she smiled as he kissed her hand. They exchanged basic information in Spanish: what home towns they were from, where they lived in New York, the names of relatives. They had absolutely nothing and no one in common, but that didn't matter. Now they knew each other in a secret way. Simon turned to me, and caught me eying the policewoman in the hall.

"You like the sights in Puerto Rico?" he said.

"Only the ones that you've hired," I said.

"What is this?" Marta said. "National *Pendejo* Week? Let's get down to business."

Simon smiled at her, and picked a sheet of ruled yellow paper off the desk.

"That woman, Rebecca Kovner?" Simon said. "She arrived in San Juan yesterday. She's not staying at any of the hotels. There were at least two other Israelis on board the plane. One of them was Ira Goldstein. American Airlines."

"Touchdown," I said.

"What's this about?" he said, his cop's nose quivering.

"I don't know yet. Let's go out and see the body."

"Good," Simon said. "We can all go in my car."

"No, Simon," I said. "Let's take both. Just in case we have to make a few stops. I'll follow you."

"Suit yourself."

He got into a blue police car and we followed him out of the lot. He drove a long way across flat, dark land. The tract developments in the clotted suburbs fell away. I turned off the air conditioner and opened the window and let the sweet night smells move around us. Marta was quiet. The road climbed, as the taillights of Simon's car bobbed along ahead of us. I could smell rotting vegetation now, thick and rich and loamy, and then suddenly it was raining and I knew we were skirting the edge of the rain forest around El Yunque, the island's highest mountain. There were no lights at all now except from our cars, and I tried to imagine what Ike's last hours on the earth had been like, whether they had tied and bound him and taken him along this same road. Or whether he had been shot in San Juan and taken out here like discarded meat to be burned in some empty wood. The windshield wipers peeled back the rain. I rolled my window halfway up, but Marta let the rain fall against her for a while.

"I didn't know this was all up here," Marta said quietly. "I always think of P.R. as flat and crowded. Beaches, not mountains."

"It's beautiful in the daylight," I said. "All lush plants and wildness. No plastics factories. No McDonalds or Burger King or Chicken Shack. Just a beautiful place, the way it was when the Taino Indians lived here."

The rain slowed and then stopped. We rolled down the windows. The air was fresh and clean and wet with the rain. Simon's car kept bobbing along ahead of us on the twisting two-lane road. No traffic came the other way. The world was asleep.

"I'd like to get out and take off my clothes and just roll in the leaves," Marta murmured. "Just feel it all wet and chocolate brown and dirty against my belly."

She sounded like a little girl in a winter classroom longing for summer.

"Maybe we can do just that," I said. "When this is over."

"Is this ever gonna be over?" she said.

"Soon," I said. "It should be over soon."

Then there were moving pinheads of white light up ahead, and Simon's taillights grew larger as he braked, and the white lights circled like fireflies, and we pulled over to the side of the road. I got out, and looked up and saw a billion stars frozen in the immense sky. The night smell was powerful now, but there was something else mixed into it, something foul, a trace of gasoline and scorched flesh.

"It's not gonna be too pretty," Simon said to Marta. "You can stay here."

"No, I'd like to see it."

Two local cops were holding the flashlights, treating Simon with the deference that is shown a man who is only temporarily out of power. One of them led the way off the road. A great wall of rock climbed from the road into the darkness above, and someone had spray-painted the words "Viva Cristo El Rey" on the most visible part of the rock-face. There were scattered beer cans and a few defiant wrappers from contraceptives. Insects muttered and chirped, but otherwise the place was quiet. Our steps made cracking sounds as we moved into the thick foliage.

"This is a lovers' lane most of the time," Simon said, translating the grunts of one of the local cops. "The kids come up from Ponce and the coast towns, and park off the road in the dark. That's why they got 'Long Live Christ' painted back there on the rocks . . ."

"I like clean sheets myself," I said.

"Oh, wow," Marta said suddenly.

The flashlights were steady now, pointing into a lush, overgrown bowl beside a small stream. Some of the surrounding plants had been scorched black. The gasoline smell was stronger. Lying on its back was the body. The face had been burned away, so that you could see some bone, white and yellow in the light, but no clear features. A stump of nose. No ears. The clothes were burned too, and some of the flesh. There were four holes in the chest. One cop came closer, grunted a few words in Spanish, and pointed to the back of the head. It had been blown off.

But it wasn't Ike.

I knew that from the great bulk of the body. It wasn't Ike Roth at all.

It was Pinchos.

20.

It was finally too much for Marta. She turned, making a small, whimpering sound in her throat, and pushed past Simon and climbed up out of the bowl and into the clearing and got sick. I stood beside her for a long time, and held her as firmly as possible. When she was finished she leaned back and gulped the night air and shivered in the chilly darkness. She looked older now. Simon told one of the cops to get the brandy from the glove compartment of his car. She sipped the brandy, and I told Simon about Pinchos. At least, part of what I knew about Pinchos. Where he lived and what his business was, and that the missing Ike Roth was his partner. The moon had pushed past El Yungue and Marta looked worse in the sallow light. I took her out to the road.

"I think you'd better go home," I said quietly.

She moistened her lips. "I came here with you. I'm going home with you. It's just like a prom. Same rules as a prom."

"I don't want you to come any further."

"Please, Sam."

"I'll be back as soon as possible. I've got one last stop to make. Do you have those pistol clips in your purse?"

"In the car," she said weakly. "In the purse, in the car."

"And the address of the finca? The one in Carmen's name?"

"That too."

I put the clips in my pocket, and then asked Simon for directions to the finca. The place was about fifteen miles away, on winding road. Simon showed me the route on a police map and then told me he would bring Marta back to the Hilton.

"You're not gonna get in any trouble, are you?" Simon said.

"If I thought I was, I'd ask you to come."

"Then why are you packing heat?" he said.

I smiled. "Ah, the eyes of a good cop." I patted the .45 under the breast pocket of the jacket. "I guess a rod makes me feel like a big man, that's why."

"I wouldn't let you go anywhere at all, if you didn't have that thing," he said.

"I just hope I don't have to use it."

Then I told him that when I had discovered the missing pieces of the story, he could have the whole case and take all the bows. Meanwhile he could look for Ike Roth. He had to trust me, and get Marta back safely to the hotel. He sighed.

"I remember you when you were just a reporter," Simon said. "What's with the guns?"

"It's family, Simon. I hope you understand."

"Oh, I understand all right. I don't like it, but I understand."

I kissed Marta on the cheek and told her where

I was going. I told her to double-lock the door in the hotel room. She nodded and got into the car. Simon said he would have someone at the hotel keep an eye on her too. I thanked him, and they pulled away, heading down the dark, narrow road to San Juan. I got into the rented Plymouth and went the other way. I wished the Plymouth wasn't white.

The lights of the finca were about a thousand yards off the road, beyond a field of sugar cane, near the sea. I parked on the shoulder and left the keys in the ignition, for a fast departure, and found a dirt path through the cane. I took the safety off the .45. There were rich earth smells down here and the sea breeze riffled the cane, and dogs barked somewhere, and in the open places I could see the distant phosphorescent glow of the Caribbean. The stars had not moved. I walked a long way.

Then the finca was before me. It was bone-white in the moonlight, a long low one-story stucco structure, with a roof of Spanish tiles, and a garden in front with vegetables growing on sticks. Shafts of yellow light streamed from the windows, spilling into the front yard. Two cars were parked to the side, a brown Ford, and a Chevy station wagon. Behind the main building there were two smaller buildings, probably a barn or a henhouse, and another house on a hill beyond, with a single bulb burning over the door. Over to the left was a standard-sized basketball court, with rows of blue lights running around the baselines. Monon must play here to stay in shape for the rigors of New York. Or maybe this was where Turtle was forced to eat dinner. I waited in the darkness of the cane, edging slowly to my left, trying to see into one of the windows.

The door opened, and a fat woman in a pink dress stepped out on the porch. She was holding a drink. I could hear music now, full of romantic guitars in the style of Los Tres Panchos. The woman leaned against a post and looked up at the stars. She had to be Monon's wife. Carmen. She looked sad and lonesome, and when she sat back on a plastic chair, she turned her toes in to touch each other like a little girl. She sat there for a long time.

Then Monon walked out onto the porch. He was shirtless and barefoot, the powerful hairless torso glistening with sweat in the light. He was zippering up his trousers. The fat woman looked at him, and then went back to her drink. He said something and smiled. She sipped the drink.

I moved around to see better.

And saw Ileana. She was in the main room of the finca, coming out of the bathroom. She was wearing a paisley robe, and her blonde hair was tousled. She stared into a mirror and started brushing the hair in short, angry strokes. Monon peered around the edge of the door at her, and then said something to the fat woman. She said nothing back. She just sipped her drink.

Then Monon tensed. He looked at the sky. I could hear a faint tump-tump-tump, and looked behind me, the cane higher than my head, and stared up at the sky. I heard it before I saw it, the thumping becoming louder, turning into the beating of an engine, the hard, steady, familiar whir of rotor blades. The blinking red landing light came into view, and Monon was inching cautiously toward the basketball court, and then I could see the helicopter.

The long fuselage was painted black, and as it hovered above us it seemed enormous, monstrous, a killer from the night. I remembered the way they had looked in Vietnam, with their guns poking from the sides, and the scared kids who manned those guns, and what they would do when they came to a place where anything moved. Now this giant black thing was coming straight down near where I was hidden, the great force of its rotor blades flattening the world, flattening the tops of trees, flattening the stalks of cane. For a moment, I stood alone and exposed, the cane around me smashed against the earth by the man-made wind, and I went down on my face, and lay there. And then the cane slowly rose again, the noise stopped, the helicopter had landed.

I didn't move. I rubbed a pinkie finger in each ear, unplugging the stuffed wads of noise and force. When I could hear the world again, I peered out through the cane.

Monon had pulled on white shoes and a *guayabera* shirt and was walking across the basketball court to the spot near the center where the copter was squatting. The rotor blades spun slowly to a stop. A door plopped down on the near side of the black fuselage, bounced off the concrete and became steps. The first man out was Latin, wearing a white T-shirt, Bermuda shorts, sneakers and a flying cap. He gave a hand to the next man. This one was young and bearded, with pale white skin, a black suit, and an eye patch like Moshe Dyan. That was Ira Goldstein.

The other passenger was a woman. The man with the patch offered her his hand, but she ignored it, and pranced down the steps, like a cold wind cutting a path through the thick, humid air. She was wearing a dark, well-cut business suit and dark shoes, and was carrying a zippered leather bag. Her bare legs were a little too straight to be perfect, but her black hair shimmered in the blue lights of the landing field, and except for the cold aura, she was beautiful. She went straight to Monon and he held out his hand. The woman shook the hand in a formal way, like a visiting diplomat. I knew she must be Rebecca.

They exchanged words, and then Monon led her to the house. The man with the patch followed, and when she entered the house, he stood at the door with his hands in front of him, like a prize-fighter in civilian clothes waiting to be introduced before a big fight. The helicopter pilot fiddled with his aircraft, and then lay flat on his back on the landing field, dozing in the humid air. Through all of this, Carmen Perez had not moved.

I was thinking about my options: rushing the place, waiting for them all to get tired, drifting back through the cane field to my car to get help from Simon, sneaking on board the helicopter and using the gun later. I wondered where Ike Roth was. I wondered if Marta was all right. I was hoping the Turtle had not followed Monon Perez to San Juan.

And then I wasn't thinking anything anymore.

There was an iron bar across my neck, and a brutal force behind me. My back was breaking, and my arms were boneless and I was swallowing my tongue. Then the world grew vague, almost dreamy, and there was nothing left in my lungs and I was going blind and then I just fell away and was gone.

21.

There were exploding little pinholes of lights. There was a bumping, rolling dream, with no pictures, no faces, no landscapes; just bumping and rolling as if I were being dragged across the bottom of the sea. There was blackness and silence and voices and a yellow explosion and then silent blackness again. And when I woke up, my mouth was full of the taste of raw meat and I could smell dirty perfume and hear the thumping of the sea tide. I tried to move my arms, but they were tied behind me. I thought I could move my fingers but I wasn't absolutely sure, because I could feel nothing. My feet were bare, my shirt and jacket off. The sea pounded in very close.

I turned my head and saw Ileana.

"You're awake, huh?" she said, in a slurred voice. "Thought you'd never wake up."

She was sitting on a bench. Behind her was a thatched wall, made of braided palm tied to a wood frame to form a shack. I moved my tongue. The taste of uncooked meat was from the blood in my mouth. I coughed up a sticky lump of blood and phlegm and spit it a few feet into the dirt. Then I rolled over on my back, dug my hands into the earth and shoved myself into a sitting position.

"You're pretty strong, aren't you?" she said, without moving. There was a burr of an accent to her voice. She was smoking a joint.

"Where is this place?" I said.

"I don't know," she said dreamily. "I know it's in Puerto Rico. Yeah, it's in Puerto Rico. And it's near the ocean." She giggled. "But where it is exactly, I don't know. I'm from New York myself."

"Me too."

"I thought Turtle broke your neck when he caught you in the cane field," she said pleasantly. "He sure is a mean guy."

"Turtle's here?"

"Yeah. He's here. He's so mean and ugly."

"Where are the others?"

"Oh, they're around," she said. "They're here. Don't worry. They didn't go no place."

"I bet you'd rather be in the Corso than right here, right now."

"I sure would. Hey! You go to Corso?"

"Only when Tito Puente's there. Or Ray Barreto."

"Hey, you really *know!*"

"How about cutting this rope?" I said hopefully. She might have been high enough to do it.

"Oh, silly," she said. "You can't go nowheres. They wanna *talk* to you."

"I don't want to talk to *them*," I said. "I want to take you to the Corso."

"You're a funny man." She took a drag on the joint. "Wanna *toke?*"

I didn't have time to reply. A door opened on the left and Monon walked in. The *guayabera* was pale blue and freshly starched. His hair was combed straight back, and something mad was dancing in his right eye, like a virus. He stood above me. His face twitched.

"Here he is," Monon said. "Wide awake. Fit as a fiddle. The big man. The big reporter. What you gonna write now, boy?" He kicked me in the arm. "Who you gonna write about now, asshole? How you gonna write your way outta this one? Huh? The big man."

He braced himself, pivoted low, and smacked me hard in the face. "Turtle wants you so bad, Briscoe. He wants to chew your face off. But maybe I'll do you myself. Just hit you till you're not alive no more and then put you in the helicopter and feed you to the sharks."

"You're losing your muscle, Monon," I said. "You're way out of shape. Fat and finished. You must have eaten too many poor people in New York."

He whipped the back of his hand across my face and was steadying himself for another shot, when the door opened again.

"Stop, you idiot."

My eyes focussed again, teary from the slapping around, and I saw Rebecca standing over me. She had a British accent, like so many of the sabras who were taught by instructors left over from the old British mandate.

"I want to talk to him alone," she said.

"Let me get it out of him," Monon said. "Or Turtle."

"You'd only kill him. And then we'd know nothing. Just wait outside." She turned to poor, dumb Ileana, who had not moved from the bench. "You too. Out."

Ileana looked surprised, smiled, got up and followed Monon outside, carrying her lush body wearily, as if it were a curse. Rebecca strode after her to the door, and said something in Hebrew. Up close, her face was beautiful: a long aquiline nose, jet black hair that swirled around her face, dark eyebrows that needed no kohl, green eye shadow, full lips, good jaw. All of this was perched on a long, thin neck that rose from square, blocky shoulders. She was not wearing a blouse under the suit jacket and when she moved I could see a dark line of cleavage. She moved with a sense of command.

The man with the eye patch handed her the leather briefcase. She put it on the bench, looked at me coldly, and lit a cigarette. The door closed and we were alone.

"Now," she said, as if the single three-letter word explained everything.

"Now what, Rebecca?"

She circled around and stood before me. Her face softened in surprise. "You know my name?"

"I know a lot of things, little girl," I said, looking up at her. "But you'll never know any of them if you kill me."

She squatted down to face me, her legs spreading peasant style, the muscles of her calves and thighs bulging strongly. I smelled a faint aroma off her, something delicate and distant, mixing in the air of the shack with the dime-store smell of Ileana.

"You have an excellent point," she said. "Outside,

they want to kill you. Our transaction is nearly complete. I have what I came for, or will have it very soon. But these people are sloppy and crude and tend to leave things a mess."

"Like the mess at Sarah Roth's house?" I said sharply.

Her face became an ugly grid. "That was a mistake. An overreaction. That heavy one, the one with the bandages on his chest . . ."

"Turtle?"

"Yes. He went with my, uh, my associate, because, after all, we don't know New York. He was to make a simple search. Either to find what we were looking for, or to determine that it was not there. He did not expect to see you there. And he did not expect that Turtle fellow to . . . to overreact."

She seemed to be maintaining her control through an act of will. She stood up and went over to the bench. She was going to tell me some of it, maybe all of it. And that meant one thing: They were going to kill me.

"And Carmelo Fischetti? What was that about?" I said.

She looked at me bleakly. "I came here to listen to you talk. Not to tell you stories."

"Let me talk then," I said. "A lot of it is very simple. Carmelo Fischetti was hit because he got greedy. He had learned from Monon that a very big deal was under way, and he tried to cut himself in. He had cut himself in on a lot of Monon's things already, and Monon wanted to get rid of him. So Monon had Ike Roth lure him to Madison Square Garden, and at the right moment had him shot. You had nothing to do with that one, Rebecca, but you had never trusted Monon. You didn't trust Ike Roth either. So that night you sent Goldstein out to Ike's house, with Turtle as a guide, to see if Ike was pulling a double-cross. And what you were after wasn't there."

She finished the cigarette, and lit another one. She said: "They told me you were a writer. You tell an amusing story."

"No," I said, "it isn't very amusing. Monon told you that the thing you wanted would be delivered by Ike Roth in Puerto Rico. You said you had the cash and would make the deal right there in New York. But Monon and Ike Roth were afraid of New York. For one thing, there are a lot of Jews in New York. You might have too many friends. You might even be working for the Israeli government, and that meant the FBI could get into the act. They wanted to move the deal to safer turf. So Ike came to Puerto Rico."

"You talk a lot, don't you?" she said.

"Only when I'm tied up," I said.

"You'll keep talking then."

"The thing you wanted was unbelievably precious and unbelievably beautiful," I said. "It was thirty-three centuries old."

Her eyes widened now.

"But you did not want just the piece itself, the breastplate of Aaron, as it's called. You wanted the man who took it from you. The man who came into your life when you were alone and seventeen and your lover was dead. The fat man who crept into your apartment one day in Tel Aviv. The man who calls himself Lev Pinchos."

"Stop," she said softly.

"That was what you were really after. You were

after Lev Pinchos. So you got a message to him after I saw him and lured him here. You tempted him with a deal. You drew him away from New York, and when you got him here, you killed him."

"Stop, please stop."

"And that was all you really wanted. To kill the fat man. And with Lev dead, that poor boy, Arieh, the Yemeni who died in the desert, proving something or other for someone or other, could rest peacefully. The gift from God was gone, but you had at least taken the life of the man who stole it."

"It was not like that!" she blurted. She stood up and circled around me, pacing quickly on those thin legs. "He was a good boy. He would not have wanted me to . . . to . . ."

I realized that she was sobbing in a dry, hurt way, her back to me, so that I couldn't see her face from where I was sitting.

"I'm glad to see that you're human," I said softly. "I didn't know you had a tear in you."

"You know nothing about me," she said, her voice hardening, her back to me.

"Maybe I know more than you could ever admit," I said. "You don't work for the Israeli government, do you? You wouldn't be involved in these killings if you did. This is strictly personal."

"You don't know what it . . . what those years were like. The years when I was alone. When I left the world and toughened myself and prepared myself for what I knew I would have to do. Years when I deprived myself of everything: companions, films, laughter, dancing, sex . . ."

"That's a shame."

She went on in a toneless voice. "You'll have to die, of course. There can be no loose ends."

"There are always loose ends, my young friend. The San Juan police know what has happened. And the San Juan police will tell the New York police and the New York police will tell the reporters. And then everyone will know. The Hasidim will know about the death of Lev Pinchos. They will know in Israel, and they will know everywhere else in the world. You cannot kill all the New York police, all the reporters, all the Hasidim, all of Israel, all of the world. They will come for you. And they'll find you."

I looked up, and something like a smile flickered on her face. Her voice was cold again.

"Perhaps the San Juan police will never be able to tell what they know," she said.

She went to the door and threw some Hebrew words into the darkness. My heart was pounding. I felt small and weak. The sea seemed to move closer. I heard a car door slam and then the heavy, foot-scraping sound that goes with the carrying of something heavy. Rebecca didn't look at me. She lit another cigarette.

The door opened. Turtle stood there, grinning at me, holding a body. He spat to the side, and heaved the body into the shack. It fell hard and rolled over on its back.

"Hello, Briscoe," Turtle said.

I looked into the face of Simon Sandino.

Insanity has its own peculiar strength. And now it roared through all of me, through every muscle and every bone, through the knotted cords of the old fighter's tendons, through legs and shoulders. There was a scream in me, that no one ever heard, and the scream said one thing: Marta. And I was up somehow, smashing into Rebecca, driven by a bloodtide of lunacy, full of that aching, murderous scream, driving her into the braided wall of the shack, driving her through it, the wall of the shack bursting and falling. Then tumbling over her.

I saw Turtle's face, and turned away, stumbling, thinking: they killed Marta too. No: I killed her, I brought her here and now she's dead. I screamed her name, but made no sound, and drove forward. Bumping into something, thinking: they killed Simon and they killed Lev Pinchos and they killed Sarah and they killed Fischetti: and they killed Marta too. I was turned, stopped, lifted, thumped. *He's a strong pubic hair*, someone said in Spanish. They killed Marta. They blew her away. And I saw Turtle again: the slush-colored eyes, the thin, mirthless grin. Arms were holding me now: I saw Monon's face: and then life just went out of me, went out through my mouth and ears and eyes, was slammed right out of me. Dead, they lifted me. *We have to kill this pubic hair*. Dead, I fell against leather. *You can't kill him unless Monon says so*. Dead, they took me somewhere, not far, bumping and hurt. Dead, I smelled Rebecca's perfume, heard Turtle's voice. I was dead for a long time. And then I was alive again, and they were pulling up in front of the finca. A car door opened. People got out.

The helicopter sat on its pad.

Carmen was gone.

One of the cars was gone.

I saw Monon.

His lips moved.

A long time later, his words entered my brain.

"Take him inside."

"Don't kill him. Not yet."

That was the girl's voice. Rebecca.

"He knows where Ike is."

That was her voice again.

A big, dark laugh.

"He doesn't know shit about Ike, lady."

That was Monon.

"What do you mean?"

Her voice again. With panic in it.

"I got Ike. I got Ike right up that hill in that little cabin, lady. And I got that piece of jewelry too."

"What?"

Her voice now. I moved. I was alive. I could move, I was lying on the back seat of the car. Turtle was leaning on the front fender, his back to me. Monon and Rebecca were ten feet away. Goldstein, with the eye patch, stood to their right. For the moment they all had forgotten me.

"Why didn't you say you had him from the beginning?" Rebecca said.

"Because I haven't seen a dime of that five million yet, sister. And I didn't want to take no chances on you pulling a fas' one."

"You'll get your money."

"I don't like these Swiss bank deals. I never go to Switzerland. I don't ski."

Turtle coughed: "Seems to me she could have something in that little leather bag."

"Why don't you take a look?" Monon said.

"Okay, boss."

He took a step and Goldstein whipped out a .45. It was one of the biggest .45's I'd ever seen. He aimed it at Turtle.

"Don't move," he said to Turtle.

"They can't take a joke, these people, can they, boss?"

Goldstein stood behind Monon, and patted him down. No guns. Then he went toward Turtle, the gun straight out in front of him. He seemed to be measuring each step, estimating the distance, trying to chart the terrain between him and Turtle.

He charted it wrong. Turtle rushed in low, and Goldstein fired, and when he did I went out the door of the car, running low, sprinting for the sugar cane. I heard another shot, and voices, and then I was into the cane, its edges slicing at me, plunging deeper. I crouched down, hugging the damp earth, and listened. I heard nothing.

I had beaten them.

I was alive.

All I had to do now was wait, and then go back and kill them all.

22.

The car. I had to reach the car. There were rifles in the trunk. And ammo. I moved through the cane, my hands still tied, avoiding the paths. Small unseen animals moved away from me, but I heard no humans behind me. I was in there for minutes or hours; I couldn't really know. And then broke out on to the road.

The car was gone.

Someone had come and taken it away. The car was gone, and the rifles were gone. And I just lay down there, in the drainage ditch beside the road, shuddering with pain and running and death. I tried to remember Marta's skin. Its smoothness on my face. Her hair. Teeth. I might have slept. I don't remember.

And then I heard a car and looked up and it was mine. A rifle was pointing from the window on the passenger side.

The lights were out. It was cruising. I ducked low. It came closer, inching along now. And I saw who was driving.

"Marta!"

The car stopped, and she looked at me, and I was up out of the drainage ditch, covered with muck, and she was looking at me, her hair tousled, her face dirty, her eyes wild, and Carmen was beside her, cradling the rifle. I stumbled, got up, felt like a drunk trying to turn a corner, and then sat down hard. The door opened.

They washed my wounds in the sea. Carmen and Marta holding me up, dragging me through the brambles and the sea grass, and then just letting me fall into the surf. I tried to get up, and they pushed me down, Carmen barking orders in Spanish, Marta giggling, as the cold morning water of the Caribbean shocked me into consciousness, and the burning, healing salt rolled over my sliced and battered body.

And then my head was clear and I could stand, wearing only trousers now, and I could walk. I felt the blood begin to surge again, clean and fresh and healthy, the adrenalin pumping hard, the need for completion moving through me, and I knew that I had to finish it off. We hurried back to the car.

"Tell me," I said. "What happened?"

"Later," she said in a flat voice.

"Now."

Carmen was driving wildly, the car's lights still out, racing down familiar back roads while Marta told me most of what had happened.

"We went only a few miles," she said, "and a car cut us off. The driver was a fat man, probably the man you call Turtle. I knew it was him. It must have been. He was holding the wheel with one hand and there was a gun in the other and he just fired. Simon must have died right away. I went low, and jerked the wheel and we went off the road, and I jumped out. And I ran. It was all jungle and I found a tree with huge roots and I went under the roots and stayed there. I heard him moving around. Once he came so close I could hear him breathe. And then he went away. I heard car doors slamming. Two sets of them. He must have taken Simon back with him, like a trophy. I stayed in the jungle, off the road, and just walked. I kept looking up for cars, but I was afraid of them too. One of them might be you, but one of them might be Turtle."

"That bastard."

"Then I saw your car, parked on the road. The keys were still in the ignition. I took them out and went down the path to the cane. There was nobody there but Carmen. I went straight to her. She told me that everybody had gone to the beach house. I asked her what the helicopter was for. She said it was for the guests. But she was drinking, and I knew then that everything was a mess. She didn't know a word of English, so I cursed her in Spanish. I told her she was a goddamn fool to put up with Monon's crap. I told her she should dump that bastard, and I would help her do it, if she helped me find you. I described you. She said you were with them. I got her steamed up real good." She laughed. "Then I gave her the high, hard one. I reminded her that all of these places were in her name. If anything happened to Monon, the whole shebang was hers. She could start over. She could marry someone decent. She could run the farms herself. I told her a whole lot of things. And she just stood up, and came right back to the car with me, and I remembered the rifles."

Carmen suddenly pulled onto a small dirt road, climbing into hills, and then swerved around and stopped. We were on a rise above the finca. The cars and the helicopter were still there, so all of them were somewhere on the grounds. And Ike Roth was probably with them. Along with that lethal piece of jewelry.

"They're not in the main house," Carmen said softly in Spanish. "They're over there. In the cabin."

She pointed to the building with the lone light bulb. It was designed like a small European hunting lodge, with a sloping gabled roof. We could see only the back of it. Carmen led the way through the foliage. I was carrying one of the rifles, and Marta had the other. Carmen had nothing. She didn't seem to care. Despite her size, she moved down those paths with the delicacy of a ballroom dancer. The foliage was dense and rubbery, wet with morning dew. The sky was beginning to lighten. Then, through a screen of foliage, I could see the helicopter pilot sitting at the edge of a small clearing, facing the cabin. He was obviously more than just a pilot. He must have been the man who spoke Spanish when they were beating me in front of the beach house.

I motioned silently for Marta to cover me, and then moved toward him. Insects hummed. Birds began calling to each other. Somewhere a hen cackled about the new day. The pilot had a shotgun tucked under his armpit like a baton. His hands were occupied with a can of beer and a cigarette.

I moved close enough to smell one lazy tendril of blue smoke. We were a hundred yards from the main house. The pilot hummed a small tune and I stepped out of the cover of the foliage.

"Hey, motherfucker," I whispered.

He turned and I swung for the upper deck.

The rifle stock hit the hinge of his jaw and he fell without a sound. I looked down at him, at his pebbly, acne-scarred face, the dirty mustache, the bubble of blood forming in his mouth, and the jaw slung an inch to the side. I wanted to feel sorry for him but I couldn't. I reached down and picked up his shotgun. I cracked it open. There were two shells in it. There were five bullets in the rifle clip. I held the shotgun in my left hand and the rifle in my right, looked around for other gunsels, saw no one, looked back to where I knew Marta and Carmen were, signaled for them to wait, and then walked across the open space on my sore city feet to the front door of the cabin.

I flattened myself against the wall beside the door and listened.

I could hear murmuring voices. One of them belonged to Ike Roth. The faces of the recently dead flashed through my mind. My heart was rapping against my throat.

I kicked open the door.

Everything blurred, and someone fired a pistol. Blam, Blam. And I rolled to my side, firing the shotgun at the sound of the pistol, heard a choked coughing sound, a woman's scream, something hard hitting the wooden floor, and I came up out of the roll with my back to the wall and the two long guns straight out and they were sitting there before me at the table like figures in a wax museum. Rebecca, her face ashen, and her jaw falling. Monon with the braces of his dentures showing as his mouth widened and then stopped at its outer limits. And Ike Roth, lashed to a chair against the chinked wall, his suit jacket creased by the ropes, his face lumpy and bruised, his eyes astonished. Everybody but Turtle.

"Don't ... fucking move," I said.

I got up and walked around the table. A lone bottle of Don Q was in front of Monon. The kitchen was modern, with a sink, stove, dishwasher, refrigerator-freezer, all shinny and new. I looked down at the body of poor Ira Goldstein. He wasn't nice to look at. The blast from the shotgun had caught him in the face. He looked like two hundred pounds of hamburger in a black suit. Turtle had let him live, but Ira just couldn't stop pulling guns.

"Hello, Ike," I said, without looking at him.

"Hello, Sam."

"Everybody's been looking for you, Ike."

"So I hear."

"Some people have died," I said. I walked away from Goldstein's body and stood in front of Ike, still holding the shotgun and the rifle.

"I know," Ike said. His eyes were the color of wood smoke and he smelled of defeat and flight and betrayal.

"I talked to Jason before I came down here," I said. I glanced over at Rebecca and Monon. They stared at me, but didn't move. Monon's face was still locked in that over-wide smile.

"What did he say?" Ike said softly.

"He was certain you were dead. And in a way, he was right. You're not Ike Roth. You're not Ike

Roth, who was faithful to his wife. You're not Ike Roth who went to a spelling bee with his son. You're definitely not Ike Roth from Brownsville." My voice sounded hoarse and grainy. "That Ike Roth must be dead. I don't know who the hell you are pal."

"Sam, I . . ."

"Shut up."

I motioned with the rifle at Monon. "Stand up, muscles."

He got up slowly, his face twitching. I motioned to the sink and the drawers beside it. "Go over there and get a knife and cut those ropes," I said. "And don't get funny, or I'll give you an extra asshole."

He walked over to the sink.

"Sam, I really had reasons," Ike said. "You don't know the half of it. I can explain all this."

"To who? Sarah? Jason? Naomi? Who you gonna explain it to, Ike? To your partner, that poor son of a bitch Pinchos? Who, Ike?"

"I was into the shylocks, Sam. We hadn't been doing too good in the business, and well, Carmelo was looking for his money. I had moved some things for him and Monon before, and this looked like a big piece of business. The kids cost me a mint at school. Everything costs a mint. I saw the possibility of a score, Sam. All of it free and clear. A score off the books."

Monon took a bread knife from the drawer. He began to saw at the thick bottom strand of ropes that were holding Ike's feet.

"I thought I had it figured good," Ike said. "Make the deal, then go away forever. With that kind of money—half of five million dollars!—I could take the kids and Sarah and just disappear. Change names. Become someone else."

"You did that, all right. You became someone else, all right."

"We had it worked out. I was supposed to come down here, meet Monon, and wait for Rebecca, who had the money. But I guess Monon didn't trust me."

One of the ropes fell away, and Ike moved his legs. Monon said: "Why the hell should I trust you?"

"You wanted it all, Monon," Ike said. "You wanted the whole five million, didn't you?"

Monon shook his head, sawing slowly on the second strand of rope, throwing a glance at the door. "Stop talkin', will you?" he said. "You sound like a goddamn canary."

Ike smiled at me. "Anyway, I got off the plane down here, and Monon had a car waiting for me to take me to the Hilton. Only they didn't take me to the Hilton. They threw some kind of rag over my face and knocked me cold, and I woke up out here. I've been here ever since." He smiled in a smarmy way. "So you see, Sam, I didn't kill anyone. I couldn't. They had me on ice."

Monon cut through the second strand. There were two more across Ike's chest, and his hands were tied separately behind the chair.

"You didn't have to kill anyone," I said. "You had these jerks do it for you. Monon got rid of Carmelo, but Rebecca here, she did the heavy work, with a little help from Turtle and our friend on the floor. They killed Sarah, trying to get the piece without paying the five million . . ."

"Who could trust such people?" Rebecca said in a flat, distant voice. "I just wanted to be certain."

"Certain?" I said. "Or was it something else? Wasn't it more like the five million being as phony as the stationery from the Israeli government?"

Monon stopped his sawing and looked at her. So did Ike. She tried out a wise, wet smile, but it didn't work. And then she bent forward, face on her fists, covered by a helmet of hair. She made an odd, moaning sound, her teeth grinding against each other, and sobbed drily. I turned to Ike.

"Where is this thing?" I said.

Ike gave me a smug look. "It's right here in the room." Rebecca stopped sobbing, and looked at Ike.

"Keep your mouth shut, Ike," Monon said. I watched the knife and kept the shotgun aimed at his face, and my finger on the trigger of the rifle.

"It's over there," Ike said flatly. "In the freezer."

I went over to the freezer, laid the shotgun on the floor, and opened the white door. There were packages of Bird's Eye frozen food, and six steaks, and a few cans of frozen orange juice. I rummaged around with my free hand, and under the steaks I found a package. It was wrapped in a Baggie, covered with frost.

Nobody said anything, as I took the package to the table. I tore open the plastic with my teeth. And then, at last, I had the piece in my hand. It was solid and heavy and ancient, and I laid it on the table. The gold was old, the jewels gleamed. It seemed to mock us all.

"So that's it," I said. I turned to Rebecca. "You think it's worth everything that happened, Rebecca? All those years of saving and denying yourself, so you could finance this moment? All the deaths?

Take a good look." I hefted the piece, with my free hand. "Where you're going, sister, you're not going to see any jewels for a long time."

"Stop! Stop it!" she said, and then suddenly whirled and threw herself at me, scratching at me, kicking, full of desperation and violence and death. I sidestepped, trying to get off a punch, but all of her was concentrated on destroying me, and she kicked, punched, scratched at me with a wild, grinding force. I had to drop the rifle, and I shoved her hard, trying to get off just one good punch.

And then Monon was coming with the knife, small and bundled up. I stepped to the side, grabbed his knife arm, and slammed him against the wall. The knife fell. I hit him in the balls. I hit him in the belly. I hit him in the kidneys and the neck and the face. He was very strong, but at last he started to fall, and I put everything on one final punch, and almost tore his head off. He fell as if I'd shot him.

But Rebecca was out the door, and the piece was gone, and I had to go after her. She raced down the hill, kicking off her shoes, the long, thin legs taking her down the path toward the main house, carrying her leather briefcase. Marta stepped out from the treeline and fired a shot into the air, but Rebecca kept running. She was heading for that helicopter.

"Watch the house!" I shouted to Marta. "Don't let Ike get out! And watch Monon!"

Marta took Carmen's hand and they hurried to the cabin. I lost sight of Rebecca as she turned around the side of the main house. I kept running, skirted the edge, came around the corner fast.

And ran into Turtle.

It was like hitting a wall. I bounced off him, and he just stood there, looking at me. Bandages showing under a checkered sports shirt. Grinning. I backed up. I could see Rebecca lying on the ground, stunned and hurt. She had run into Turtle too. He had her leather bag in his hand, and he was twirling it.

"You're gonna love dying, Briscoe," he said. "It's gonna be some relief."

I looked around for a rock, a bat, anything. But Carmen had been a good groundskeeper. The earth was nude.

He took a step, and I ran. First to the left, then to the right, zigging, zagging, dodging around a tree, coming around to Turtle's left. He crouched, like the wrestler he had been, hands out, waiting to make contact. But I was around him, and sprinted for the helicopter. There had to be something there. A wrench. Pipes. A flare gun. Something.

I climbed into the cockpit, scrambled for something to hit him with, and found a fire extinguisher. It was painted yellow, and weighed about ten pounds. I sat in the cockpit, three feet off the ground, and looked for Turtle. He hadn't followed me. He was at the edge of the basketball court. He had Rebecca by the hair and was dragging her along the ground. She seemed barely conscious. He was still carrying the briefcase.

"Hey, Briscoe, you forgot the Jew broad," he shouted. "You just left her behind, Briscoe. And that's a cryin' shame."

He let her fall. She started to sit up, like a stunned fighter whose brain was out, but whose body was still moving. He reached down and ripped open her jacket. Her breasts were bare now.

"Whatta ya say, Briscoe," he shouted, the smile turned into a leer. "Let's make it up, and we'll *both* ball the Jew broad."

I stepped out of the helicopter, holding the fire extinguisher. My legs were unsteady. I didn't have much fight left in me. And not long ago, Rebecca Kovner had tried to destroy me. But I couldn't let Turtle do what he was thinking of doing to her.

"Leave her alone, Turtle," I said.

"I don't think so," he said, and yanked the jacket back and down, so that her arms were pinned behind her, and useless. He put the briefcase down, grabbed her hair again, and lifted her. I moved closer and could hear her groan.

"Come on, Briscoe, let's make her really groan," he said. I moved closer, and she turned, her eyes suddenly large and frightened. He bent her head back and her face twisted in pain. "Let's bury our beef. In her."

"Let her go," I said.

And he did. He dropped her, and came at me like an enraged water buffalo. It was all timing now. I waited and then swung the fire extinguisher. It hit him in the skull, and made a donging sound. He stopped, and then skittered to the side and fell over. I dropped the extinguisher and walked over to Rebecca, who was lying with her face in the concrete of the basketball court, crying and helpless. I picked up the briefcase.

And then Turtle started getting up.

Slowly.

In sections.

Looking at me.

I left Rebecca there and broke for the helicopter. Finally, Turtle stood up all the way. I jumped into the pilot's seat, shoved the briefcase under me, and fiddled with the pitch stick, the terror rushing through me as I shoved plugs and switched switches. I tried to remember all those things that the pilots had done in Vietnam. And finally something turned over. An engine. Cylinders. Something. And I forced the pitch stick forward and the helicopter started to move. I looked out the window, but the horizon wasn't where it was supposed to be. I heard the whine of the rotor blades and suddenly saw Marta coming around the side of the main house, carrying the rifle. Rebecca was over to my left, face down, very still. And the helicopter was moving. But I had done something wrong. The angle was wrong. I wasn't going forward. I was going over, with the rotor blades beating wildly.

And then I saw Turtle in front of me. A look. A flash.

And his head was gone.

Just like that.

His body was standing up, with blood pumping furiously between the shoulder blades. But his head was gone.

And then there was a grinding screech of metal, breaking glass, things tearing and bending and popping, and the world was upside down, and there were lights flashing, and a tremendous shudder, and I was on my back in the cockpit, lying on the ceiling. The helicopter was upside down, and fire was pouring from somewhere.

I rolled out the door, fell a few feet to the ground, stood up and ran. Marta was running to me.

Then I was knocked down, and so was Marta, and a deafening noise broke the dawn.

When I got up again, the helicopter was a twisted, smoldering pile of metal. I could see Turtle's body over on the right, lying still, his life bleeding onto the concrete. I couldn't see Rebecca. Marta grabbed my arm.

"Oh, Sam. Oh, Sam. Oh, Sam."

She sounded like Sarah Roth on that night that now seemed a hundred years ago and I started walking her back to the house. Then I saw Rebecca. She was face up beside the cane field. Her arms were still pinned behind her back, but her skirt had been blown off by the explosion and she was dead. I walked over and looked at her face. Her eyes were wide open, but her neck was broken. She had a beautiful body. It hadn't done anyone any good. Not even her.

Ileana was sitting on the ground outside the cabin, a few feet from the unconscious pilot. She looked up and smiled a junkie's smile. She must have walked all the way from the beach. Or maybe she took a cab. I was too tired to ask. Marta and I walked into the room. Carmen was sitting in front of the shiny new refrigerator, with the rifle pointed at the unconscious Monon. Poor Monon had missed everything.

Marta led me to a chair, but I couldn't handle it. I sat down on the floor and leaned against the wall. I tried to raise my arm to hold her hand, but it wouldn't reach.

And then I saw Ike.

He was still sitting there in his chair, like a gaunt

roped Buddha. I felt giddy and light and started to laugh. Ike. My cousin Ike.

"Ike, remember that time we followed Carl Furillo out of Ebbets Field, and the son of a bitch wouldn't give us an autograph?"

"Yeah," he said, his mouth trembling. "Yeah, but Cookie Lavagetto gave us one. Cookie was regular."

"We spent all our money on hot dogs and soda," I said, giggling. "We had to walk all the way to Brownsville."

"Do I remember?" he said. "How could I forget? It was the longest walk of my life."

"I don't think they believed us when we got home, until we showed them the autograph."

"Yeah, that day Cookie Lavagetto saved our ass."

"We were a long way from home, Ike."

"Yeah," he said. "A long way from home."

I looked over to the left.

Marta was running water in the sink, holding a towel under the faucet. I stared at the floor and then Marta came over and started sponging my face.

"Where do you think that goddamn thing is?" Marta said.

"What thing?"

"That piece of jewelry. The breastplate of Aaron."

"Henry Aaron," I said. "It belonged to Henry Aaron. Of Milwaukee, Atlanta and Boston." She shoved the damp towel between my back and the wall. I felt drunk and stupid. "It's gone," I said. "It just blew up."

"It did?" Ike said.

Marta turned to him. Her clothes were dirty from the long night and her hair was frizzing up.

"It was in the helicopter," I said. "It blew up."

"Goddamn," she said.

"There's nothing left out there?" Ike said.

"There's nothing left of anything out there, Ike. Just like there's nothing left of you."

"Sam, I had reasons."

"Yeah? Tell them to the cops."

Then poor, dumb Ileana appeared in the door. She looked sleepy and blurry and a hundred years old.

"Everybody's asleep out there," she said. "Everybody's asleep."

23.

I called the cops and then woke up Bob
Friedman at the *Star* and gave him as much as I
could tell him. Soon the cops were all over the
finca, along with the men with the cameras, and
the ambulances, and the people from the morgue.
They charged Monon with murder and conspiracy
and a few other things. They booked the pilot too,
and sent Ileana to a psycho ward. They drove us
all to San Juan in police cars, and made me go over
the story three times. They brought in Nelson
Perez and asked him a lot of questions. They
notified the New York cops. They called the Israeli
Consulate, who confirmed that Rebecca Kovner
and Ira Goldstein were not working for the government. They put Ike in a cell and charged him with
a lot of things, including conspiracy to murder.
They went over the wreckage of the helicopter,
but the briefcase had been on top of the fuel
tanks and nothing at all had survived of the Breastplate of Aaron. They had a hero's funeral for
Simon Sandino. His ex-wife was there along with
the new governor. I passed. Simon would not come

back to life if I went to his funeral. The cops were very efficient, but I never discovered whether they found Turtle's head.

Then they let us hide in a hotel in Fajardo, down the coast, and for that first long day, I didn't talk at all and neither did Marta. We broiled in the sun and ate too much and lolled in the healing sea and then slept without making love.

That night I dreamed again, but when I woke up sweating and cold I couldn't remember the details, and I turned to Marta and slept again. The next day the San Juan cops said that Ike Roth wanted to talk to me.

"Ike Roth is dead," I said.

"But he—"

"Just tell him I said that. He'll understand."

On the fifth day, just before dawn, Marta and I left the hotel and drove slowly up to El Yunque. It was raining very hard, the way it had been that first dark night when we followed Simon into the mountains to see a body. We parked the car at the side of the road and walked for a long time. Then we took off our clothes and rolled together on the floor of the empty rain forest. The only sounds came from the insects and the tree frogs. After a while, it began to rain, and we lay there naked, facing the hidden sky, and let the big, wet, half-dollar drops hammer us to the earth.

ABOUT THE AUTHOR

Born in Brooklyn in 1935, PETER HAMILL left high school after two years to become a sheet-metal worker in the Brooklyn Navy Yard. In 1952 he joined the Navy. Later he studied painting on the G.I. Bill at Pratt Institute and Mexico City College, worked as a designer and started writing for newspapers in 1960. Formerly a columnist for the New York *Post*, he now contributes to the New York *Daily News* and other papers, and has also appeared in many major magazines. He is the author of *A Killing for Christ* (1968), *Irrational Ravings* (1971), *The Gift* (1973), *Flesh and Blood* (1977) and *Dirty Laundry* (1978). He has lived in Mexico, Spain, Italy and now lives again in Brooklyn. He has two daughters, Adriene and Deidre.

A Special Preview of
the startling opening pages of
the first book starring Sam Briscoe

DIRTY
LAUNDRY

by Pete Hamill

1

I was lying on the couch in the loft, watching the fresh snow gather on the panes of the skylight and listening to Charlie Parker play "Ornithology," when the phone rang.

The button was blinking on the second line so I didn't answer it. That's the number I give to magazine editors and politicians and for them I am never home. At least not the first time they call. Besides, Bird was riding into the old sad geometrics, pulling me back to a New York that wasn't there anymore. I waited for the service to pick up. They were supposed to pick up after three rings. They picked up on the ninth. By then, I was back in the Cedar Bar in some lost year in the Fifties, when everybody talked about Pollock and bop, and the painters stood beside the poets at the bar, and the girls came out of the cold of University Place with snow melting on the shoulders of their camel's hair coats and everybody I knew was young, including me.

The phone rang again. This time it was the main line and I picked it up.

"Yeah?"

"Mr. Briscoe, it's the service. Sorry to bother you, you know, but a Miss Fletcher called on the second line and she, uh, sounded like it was urgent. She was, uh, *upset*."

"Anne Fletcher?"

"Uh, that's right. She said you knew her. She said you were old friends."

"She leave a number?"

"She did. She said she'd be there another half hour."

I wrote the number on a pad beside the phone, thanked the operator, and hung up.

Anne Fletcher.

Jesus Christ.

I flipped the pencil into the fireplace and went to the kitchen and dropped some ice into a frosted glass. I poured some John Jameson over the ice and splashed it with some water and took a pretty good belt, listened to the music, drained the glass, and then did it again.

Six years was a long time. If you were fighting a war. Or building a house. Or painting a picture. It wasn't very long at all if it involved kicking the memory of a woman. But after a long time I had finally kicked Anne Fletcher, the way some people kick cigarettes, and others kick smack. Cold turkey is never pleasant, not if you've come to love the habit. But I had done it. Of course there were times, off in some strange place, when her face would come to me at an odd hour of the night. Or I would pass a store window and see a book we'd read together and argued about, and I would remember fragments of sentences, verbal parries, ferocious thrusts, vicious one-liners, and the laughter later. Or I would see a woman strolling Fifth Avenue on a day crisp with spring, shiny brown hair bouncing as she walked, and I would move more quickly, rehearsing the words of greeting in my head, writing the dialogue, rewriting it, trying out the lines; until I passed the woman and it wasn't Anne Fletcher. It wasn't ever Anne Fletcher. Anne Fletcher was in Europe. Or Acapulco. Or out on the Coast. Anne Fletcher was gone off. Anne Fletcher was just another girl I used to know.

Goddamn her.

I went back to the living room. The record had finished playing, so I turned on WRVR and listened to Clark Terry play "Air Mail Special" for a while, and had some more of the Jameson, and walked to the front of the loft, and looked out at the snow as it fell steadily through the grimy alleys of SoHo. Then I went back to the phone, looked at the pad and dialed the number. After two rings, someone picked it up, but didn't say hello.

"Annie?" A pause. Nothing. "Annie, it's Sam Briscoe."

"Oh, Sam. Thank God you called. I've been trying to find you for two days."

It was her voice all right, and she wasn't in good shape.

"Two days, huh?" I didn't mention the

six years, but I thought about them. "Well, what's up?"

"I've got to see you, Sam."

"I don't think that's such a good idea, Annie. What's done is done."

"It's got nothing to do with that, or with us, Sam," she said. Her voice still sounded the way it always did, as if she were trying to disrobe you, purring and sibilant, an instrument of seduction fashioned in the Iowa School of Proper Young Ladies. "I'm in trouble."

"Look in the classified section of *The Voice*, Annie. They have clinics for everything these days."

"I'm not in that kind of trouble."

"Then try a shrink."

I could sense her swallowing hard on the other end of the line. Then softly: "Wow, Sam. You really are bitter."

"Nah, I'm not bitter. I'm thirty-eight."

I was trying to tell her to hang up and get out of my life, but she wouldn't listen.

"Sam, I'm scared to death."

There was a thin wire of panic in her voice, and I said, more softly now: "Tell me what it's about."

"I can't talk on the phone."

"So. It's about money."

"Money. Banks. A killing." She paused. "But I can't explain over the phone. I've got the proof. I've got the papers. I just can't talk." Another pause. "They're everywhere, you know. If they haven't bugged my phone, then they've bugged yours for sure. They can do anything. They can get anyone . . ."

She sounded as if she'd contracted a good dose of second-grade old-fashioned galloping paranoia.

"Who are they?"

"Can I meet you somewhere and tell you?"

"It's snowing out, love."

"Do you still go to that place on First Avenue?"

She meant Billy's, near 52nd Street. We'd had dinner there the first night we'd slept together.

"I go there once in a while, Annie."

"Meet me there."

"Jesus, Annie, it's already ten o'clock."

"Please, Sam. I can be there in half an hour."

I tried to sound weary and busy, but I didn't really mean it.

"Okay. Billy's, on First Avenue and 52nd Street. At eleven."

"See you," she said.

And hung up.

2

I decided to leave Red Emma home and make
my way uptown by cab. Red Emma is a car. A
beautiful, sleek Jaguar XJ-5, with V-12 engine,
eye-level warning light array, precision cast
aluminum inlet manifolds, and the temperament of a chorus girl. She and the loft were
the products of The Week of the Big Score.
One week I was in Saigon, with $6,500 in expense money from a certain magazine, waiting
for the North Vietnamese tanks to smash
down the gates of the Presidential Palace. The
following week I was in Vegas. The war was
finally over and I wasn't going to see any dead
people in that part of the world for a long long
time and I was alone and happy and started
shooting craps. When I left Vegas three days
later I had $108,000 in my pocket and had
permanently retired from gambling. My first
day home I bought Red Emma in a place on
57th Street and then realized there were very
few places in the city where I could park her
without kids carving their names into her

shoulder blades. So I found The Loft, down on Spring Street in the neighborhood called SoHo. It's a good neighborhood, a run-down grimy place where all the bankrupt 19th-century factory buildings have started to fill up with painters and sculptors and a few writers. The restaurants are good, the saloons are peaceful, and you can walk to the Village or to the Bowery depending upon how you feel that day about the nature of the human race. I picked my building because it has a freight elevator, run by a guy named Chamaco, that takes all of Red Emma. At night I park her in my living room.

The trouble with Red Emma is that she's a thoroughbred. She doesn't run well on a lousy track. Rain slows her, and snow stops her completely. So with the snow falling heavily I walked over to West Broadway and caught a cab.

"It's a bitch out there," the cab driver said.

"Yeah."

"It's a real son of a bitch."

"It is."

"If I didn't own this rig I'd pull it in."

"Shitty weather for driving, all right."

"I been in Brooklyn. I don't get that Brooklyn. Twenty years I been driving and I don't get that Brooklyn. I don't get where anything is. I don't get the people."

"I'm from Brooklyn."

"Sorry. But you know what I mean. Even in Brooklyn they don't get Brooklyn."

"You're not gonna tell me that only the dead know Brooklyn, are you?"

"What?"

"Nothing. A dumb thing some writer said once."

Billy's hadn't changed. It was one of those small excellent New York restaurants that had never been taken up by a clique, and so had never had the bad fortune of being ruined. People ate there who had eaten there thirty years ago, and nothing could happen to wreck it except its sale to some corporate gang of restaurant managers. The windows were steamy, the tables crowded, and the decor was still all chased mirrors, mahogany paneling, red and white checkered tablecloths, sawdust on the floor and Yugoslav waiters. The steaks were good and the cole slaw was the best on earth. I don't know why, but I hadn't been there for a long time. The bar was jammed with people waiting for tables.

"Mister Briscoe!"

Yuri came at me from the kitchen, his hand out in greeting, his hair thinner, looking heavier in one of the small golden jackets the waiters all wear there. He acted as if the crowd at the bar didn't exist.

"Hello, Yuri."

"It's been a long time," he said, smiling a broad Slavic smile.

"Too long. Do you have a table?"

"You alone?"

"I'm expecting someone."

He looked pleased. "Two, then."

His eyes darted around the crowded restaurant. An elderly couple was getting up from a table against the back wall. The man held the woman's chair, and helped her on with her coat. They seemed to like each other. It was that kind of place.

"It'll be just a minute," Yuri said.

"Fine."

"Where you been?"

"Oh, around," I said. "Mostly out of town."

"You don't write for the paper anymore?"

"Nah, Yuri."

"How come?"

"Too old. I retired."

"Too old? I'm too old. You're not too old."

"Reporters are people who get sent places to be pushed around by the cops, Yuri. I'm too old for that."

He laughed and led me to the table.

"John Jameson with a splash, right?"

"You do have a memory, Yuri."

He went to the bar and I sat with my back against the wall, staring at the Fresh Bay Scallops sign, and wondering why I was there.

An hour later I was on my fourth Jameson and Anne Fletcher still hadn't shown up. I had left the number on the pad beside the phone and no Anne Fletcher was listed in the Manhattan, Brooklyn or Queens telephone books. I didn't try the Bronx; nobody lives in the Bronx anymore. And if she had been in Staten Island she would have said so; to Anne Fletcher living in Staten Island would have been like settling in Kenya. She could not have kept it a secret.

Ten minutes before the kitchen closed, I ordered a medium sirloin and some extra cole slaw and another Irish and tried to fight down my anger. She was late. But then she had always been late, and there was no reason to think she'd changed. She was even late for breakfast when she served it in bed and she was always late for parties and she had never seen the first ten minutes of any Broadway show. The first couple of months we were together I thought the lateness was part of her act. She wanted to be an actress then; all the young women wanted to be actresses then, to become someone else at least once a day, in her case someone who hadn't grown up in Iowa with a pain in the ass mother and a drunken insurance man father. I first thought that she had read in some fan magazine that Marilyn Monroe was always late, so if she was going to be a big famous actress then she would have to start being late too. But it was more than that. Anne Fletcher was one of those girls out of the great Midwest who were knocked permanently off-center the day they arrived in New York and never fully recovered. She was so goddamned beautiful that I learned to relax and forget the lateness, and so did everyone else who knew her. She was

so goddamned beautiful I should have known
the day I met her that she would end up
breaking my goddamned heart.

I ate the steak in silence, watching the
snow fall on First Avenue. There is no jukebox in Billy's and no strolling musicians and
no television set, so the sounds are always
human: people murmuring, complaining, lying, seducing, consoling. But it was late now
and the place was starting to empty. The
parked cars in the street were crowned by
two inches of snow. I finished the steak and
ordered an Irish coffee.

Then I remembered the answering service. I don't know why I hadn't thought of it
earlier; the Irish part of me is slow. They had
taken her number. They might still have a
record of it. I went to the bar, broke a dollar
for change, went to the wall phone and dialed
the service. There were six fresh calls for me,
but none from Anne Fletcher. I asked them to
look around for the number she had left earlier. They found it. This time I looked at it
more carefully. It was a Brooklyn exchange.

I dialed. The line was busy.

I went back to the table and sipped the
Irish coffee. It had cooled off and tasted too
sweet now and very thick. I'd have to do a
hundred pushups to work off half the meal.

I dialed again. Still busy.

I asked Yuri to bring me a brandy, with
some soda and ice on the side. He looked at
me with something like pity, but he didn't say
anything. Maybe something really had hap-

pened to her. Money. Banks. A killing. And, of course, the ever-present "they." Every nut who ever called a city desk after midnight said "they" were after him. But Annie had papers. Sweet Annie had proof. It sounded like one of those lousy Fifties movies she wanted so desperately to be part of, years ago, when we were young.

I dialed again and this time it rang through.

"Hello? Who is speaking?"

A husky female voice with a faint Latin accent.

"Who's this?" I said.

"Who is this?" she said.

"I want to talk to Anne Fletcher."

"Who *are* you?"

"Hey, what the hell is this? An interrogation?"

She hung up.

I stared at the receiver and then looked around. Yuri and another waiter were watching me sadly.

I dialed again.

"Hello? Who is speaking?"

"Listen, I'm sorry," I said. "You have nothing to do with this. But I've been waiting for Anne Fletcher for more than two hours. It's snowing out and I'm half-drunk and pissed-off and didn't really want to see her in the first place, and I just want to find out what the hell is going on."

"Oh, my God. You must be the reporter."

"Briscoe's the name."

"Oh, my God. *Ay Dios mio.*"

Her voice drifted away.

"Hey, what is going on? Where's Anne?"

"It's too late," she said. "It's all too late."

"Too late for what?"

"For Anna. She's dead."

Sam, while tracking down Anne's killer, uncovers a missing bank with laundered money, gets involved with a torrid Mexican femme fatale and finds a trail of violence and death.

Now read the complete Bantam Book, available where paperbacks are sold.

WHODUNIT?

Bantam did! By bringing you these masterful tales of murder, suspense and mystery!

☐	10706	**SLEEPING MURDER** by Agatha Christie	$2.25
☐	11915	**THE MYSTERIOUS AFFAIR AT STYLES** by Agatha Christie	$1.95
☐	12192	**THE SEVEN DIALS MYSTERY** by Agatha Christie	$1.95
☐	12247	**THE SECRET ADVERSARY** by Agatha Christie	$1.95
☐	11926	**POIROT INVESTIGATES** by Agatha Christie	$1.95
☐	12078	**POSTERN OF FATE** by Agatha Christie	$1.95
☐	12355	**THE SPY WHO CAME IN FROM THE COLD** by John LeCarre	$2.50
☐	12443	**THE DROWNING POOL** by Ross Macdonald	$1.95
☐	11240	**THE UNDERGROUND MAN** by Ross Macdonald	$1.75

Buy them at your local bookstore or use this handy coupon for ordering:

Bantam Books, Inc., Dept. BD, 414 East Golf Road, Des Plaines, Ill. 60016

Please send me the books I have checked above. I am enclosing $_____
(please add 75¢ to cover postage and handling). Send check or money order
—no cash or C.O.D.'s please.

Mr/Mrs/Miss_____

Address_____

City_____State/Zip_____

BD—1/79

Please allow four weeks for delivery. This offer expires 7/79.

RELAX!
SIT DOWN
and Catch Up On Your Reading!

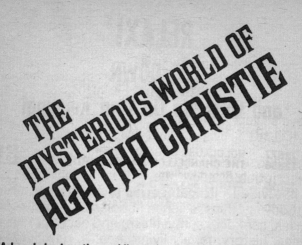

THE MYSTERIOUS WORLD OF AGATHA CHRISTIE

Bantam Book Catalog

Here's your up-to-the-minute listing of over 1,400 titles by your favorite authors.

This illustrated, large format catalog gives a description of each title. For your convenience, it is divided into categories in fiction and non-fiction—gothics, science fiction, westerns, mysteries, cookbooks, mysticism and occult, biographies, history, family living, health, psychology, art.

So don't delay—take advantage of this special opportunity to increase your reading pleasure.

Just send us your name and address and 50¢ (to help defray postage and handling costs).

BANTAM BOOKS, INC.
Dept. FC, 414 East Golf Road, Des Plaines, Ill. 60016

Mr./Mrs./Miss_____

(please print)

Address_____

City_____ State_____ Zip_____

Do you know someone who enjoys books? Just give us their names and addresses and we'll send them a catalog too!

_____

Mr./Mrs./Miss_____

Address_____

City_____ State_____ Zip_____

Mr./Mrs./Miss_____

Address_____

City_____ State_____ Zip_____

FC—9/78